143 – FOREVER AND ALWAYS

Lorie Webb

Raider Publishing International

New York   London   Cape Town

Cover images courtesy of istockphoto.com. Design inspired by the work of Ashley Webb

ISBN: 978-1-61667-171-6

Published By Raider Publishing International
www.RaiderPublishing.com
New York London Cape Town
Printed in the United States of America and the United Kingdom

Dedicated to my daughter, who inspires me through her courage and kindness.

Author's Note

I hope that you will have as much pleasure reading *143 –
Forever and Always* as I had writing it, and if you do, you
will be able to follow Lorie Finnighan and her two faithful
companions, Baberuth and Lady in the sequel *143 – More
Than Life* to see what happens next.

143 – ALWAYS AND FOREVER

Lorie Webb

Prologue

"Hello, am I speaking to Lorie Webb?"

"Who are you?" asked Lorie.

"I am a doctor from Prestige Hospital in Lagos. Their taxi has had an accident and they are critical."

"Who are you? Who are they? How did you get this number?" questioned Lorie, agitated.

"I am Dr. Devraw and your husband has had an accident," said the man.

"You are lying…"Lorie said back to the man.

"I am not; your husband and your son are critical."

"What are their names?" she asked suspiciously.

"Curtis and Joshua," answered the man.

"I want to speak to Curtis," demanded Lorie.

"He is not well right now; call back later," the man told Lorie.

I
New Beginnings

1

Autumn 2010

Lorie was sitting in her office at her computer making job applications as she had just closed a deal to leave her previous company, PC Anywhere Gmbh, a German technology company where she had been working in finance for the last couple of years. The constant commuting between Munich and Berlin and the recent acquisition of her company had taken a serious toll on her, and she had made the decision to seek a new venture that would allow her to sleep in her own bed every night.

She loved her little Bavarian hole and enjoyed her peaceful country life with her golden retriever, Baberuth. Her daughter had left to go to university in the UK at the end of the summer that year, and she felt that she had reached a place in her life where she wanted to enjoy life more and, God have mercy, not work so much; since her husband of sixteen years had tragically died of an aneurism without warning, all she felt she had done was work and nothing else to keep life going.

As she was on her computer sending out her resume to potential employers, she came up with the idea that, now that she had a little more time for herself, she should look at expanding her social circle a little more as, evidently, there was plenty of room there for improvement. For sure, that would require some effort on her part, as she was quite happy getting on, on her own, and pretty satisfied with the companionship that her dog was providing her with. It was a simple, uncomplicated relationship with no surprises, no dirty socks or shirts to iron, putting aside the dirty paws and dog's hair everywhere. Lorie did not let that worry her, as she viewed it as little inconvenience compared to the wonderful loyalty and love she was getting back from Baberuth; furthermore, he never complained about her cooking, loved it a little too much, in fact, as her dinner had many times mysteriously vanished when she was not looking. On those occasions, she would go for a back-up option, which resulted in a bowl of Cornflakes. Life with Baberuth was, all in all, simple, loving and kept her slender.

Lorie took life as it came to her and simply gave up on trying to plan it, after her husband checked out on her on a sunny Sunday afternoon shortly after they had discussed the buying of a house in Florida, as the *plan* at the time was to retire to the sunshine state. Following that event, Lorie adopted a 'no plan' philosophy and went with the flow, which she found far less stressful.

2

econnections

How does one expand her social circle when one is forty-five years of age, works all God-sent hours and seems to have barely any time to even call her own mother and daughter, she asked herself.

Moving her mouse around her laptop, she realised that, if she was going to change something regarding her current status, she needed to be bold, and started an elimination process in her head.

She was not a crowd person and did not drink, so night clubbing and bar crawling got struck off the list.

Joining a gym, maybe? She had already joined a fitness club. A *ladies only* fitness club, as she could not bear the thought of some guy checking her backside in the keep-fit class...*Yuk!* What a thought!

Golf, maybe? Been there, started that...Too much money... Too much time... and her golf bag standing to attention in the corner of her office like a roman statue was the only thing that she had left from her short-lived golfing days. Golf was deleted off the list of options.

Ballroom dancing lessons? Lorie enjoyed dancing and had always wanted to learn couple dancing. *Hmmm*, she thought. *Now here is an interesting prospect.* She opened her web browser and typed the proverbial www.Google.com address. The Mecca of all information, apparently.

"Hey! How about that?" she exclaimed.

Looking at the screen, she learnt that there was a ballroom dance school in the next town. Encouraged by this positive finding, she went to the dancing school website address and studied the various programmes meticulously, as well as the schedule of the classes. As she was running down the list, her excitement got extinguished as fast as it got fired up, as it became clear to her that, due to the time of the classes, this would definitely not be compatible with her schedule once she had resumed work life.

What was she thinking, anyway? She had a hard enough time fitting her gym time as it was. *Oh! Well...nice idea,* she thought. *But not this time around.*

She closed the browser and stared blankly at the screen for a while.

What else? *How does one living such an antisocial life get to expand their social horizon,* she kept asking herself. Staring at her open email box in front of her, she noticed one of the pop-up ads, which would usually drive her crazy. She looked at it, and turned it over in her head for a minute or two.

"Here goes nothing!" she said.

Internet Dating! She had contemplated that option in the past, but could not get herself to really go through with it, as, in her own mind, it felt too much like shopping on eBay for hardware.

But hey! Nothing dared, nothing gained, she thought. So she took a deep breath and logged onto *econnections.de.*

"No way!" she shouted, as she discovered that, unless she registered, she could not exactly run a search. *That is pure entrapment,* she thought.

She stared at the webpage for a couple of minutes and started the gruelling registration process.

QUESTION*:* Are you seeking a man or a woman?
ANSWER: A man.
QUESTION: Are you a man or a woman?

What kind of sick question is that, she asked herself.

ANSWER: A woman, of course!

At least, last time I checked. She laughed.

Email address was the next piece of information required. Hmmm, she was not to keen on revealing that part, but okay. She could not be bothered to create a new one for the occasion, so she typed, in the box, her email information.

She then had to tick a box, next to which was written: 'I accept the terms & privacy policy.'

What if she did not accept the terms and privacy policy? *Idiots,* she thought. What choice would she have…? Pfff… What a circus!

She then had to decide on what login name she would have. *That's better,* she thought. A little bit more private and secure, which made her feel more comfortable with the whole concept.

"Right, what should I use, then?" she asked Baberuth, who was lying at her feet.

How about Finnighan65? No. Too revealing. Bayern2010? How cliché! Then she remembered her car.

Her car was one of her treasures, as it was so over budget. After she was given her marching papers and a big cheque following a merger with the company she had actually relocated from the UK to Germany with, she had decided to go absolutely wild and signed a contract for a twin-top convertible with all the bells and whistles included. When one is in his or her forties, one needs to have a convertible; it is all part of the mid-life crisis process and, like puberty, one needed to be serious about their mid-life crisis. The convertible was her own statement to the world that she was over forty and proud of it! So her log in name would be Dahlfi65! She liked that idea very much.

After having made such a key decision, she went on dutifully completing pages and pages of questions, questions and more questions:

Are you tall or short? Blond, brunette or bald? Fat or skinny? Except they worded it as 'trained' or 'normal'. *How sensitive,* she thought. Do you like romantic diners or fast food? Are you the outdoor or indoor type? Are you a people person or antisocial? Do you see yourself living in a mansion or in a trailer park? More and more questions.

"Man!" she exclaimed. "How many more pages are there?"

Finally, she hit the last question and found herself confronted, this time, with a blank box where she had to write about herself and what she was looking for.

She looked down at her dog for inspiration and courage, realising that, for the first time, she was really asking herself what she would really want in a partner. It was a question she had never really thought about, and a somewhat very daunting one.

She could not quite bring herself to type in her Mr. Perfect wish, as she really had no clue at all. She skipped the big empty box and moved on to the next one.

In the next box, she had to write an introduction of herself, which would attract potential applicants. It felt to her as if she was either recruiting someone for a job or putting herself up for sale like a detergent product. As she was going into this on tip toes and was not quite sure whether she liked the idea of canvassing for a relationship on the Internet, she decided to keep it simple, light hearted, but still straight to the point.

Hi, everyone, I need to point out that my German-speaking skills are a huge construction site, so I am a lot more comfortable in English for now, unless someone can help me out here. It would be great to meet a special companion to do fun things to start with. One of my wishes would be to learn to dance the traditional ball room dances, as well as the more fun Salsa type of dance. So if your feet are burning, too, let me know.

That should do it, she thought. Anyway, she was not going to take it too seriously, but it might give her a little distraction, nonetheless, and take her mind off the fact that she needed to get a new job quickly.

As she looked at Baberuth, who was giving her the 'C'mon, woman, let's go already' look, it sprang to her mind that maybe this would also be a good time to provide Baberuth with a companion, too.

Eventually, she would be going back to work, and the old boy was getting lazier each day, looking more like a luxury rug than a dog, as he spent most of his time sleeping away. So a little friend would be good company for him whilst she was at work and would maybe give him an incentive to move his big butt, as Jane, Lorie's daughter, used to say.

Lorie made a mental note to research it. She put her laptop on snooze mod and went back up the stairs to the hallway, put on her ski suit and woolly hat, and walked out into the cold November air with Baberuth. There was snow on the ground, which reminded her that Christmas was just around the corner and Mother would be coming to town.

3

Mother

Lorie had not revealed to her mother the fact that she was officially jobless, as she did not want to cause the old lady any concerns. Her mother was somewhat a drama queen and extremely emotional, not in a loud theatrical way, but more in a quiet way, as per she would express her anxieties through the tone of her voice and the faces she pulled. Lorie could interpret her mother like an open book and had a hard time dealing with those motherly emotional moments.

Since Lorie's husband had passed away, she had skilfully manoeuvred around her mother in order to not let the old lady know of all her troubles, worries and pains, no matter what. Over time, she had closed up on her mother and she kept their once a week telephone conversations very generic, like discussing the weather, the neighbours, the family, Baberuth, etcetera...

When Jane ended up in hospital, she found it extremely difficult to try to manage the emotions of her mother, let alone the time when Lorie, herself, had ended up in the emergencies due to a physical breakdown driven by overworking, stress and exhaustion.

Nope, no way should her mother be aware of her unemployed status and, this time around, she would not even bring her daughter into confidence, her daughter, with whom she would usually discuss her troubles and even partner with in hard times, usually to plan out how they would handle Mother in certain situations.

Mother was always a very big topic of conversation between Lorie and Jane.

Jane was in a second year at university and Lorie was not going to do anything that would defocus Jane on her studies. Mother and Jane were coming over for Christmas, and Lorie was going to make it the best Christmas she possibly could whilst doing her best to preserve her secret.

As she had taken barely any holidays prior to leaving her firm, it was easy to get past Mother that she had obtained the whole two weeks over Christmas off. Lorie was looking forward to spending some well overdue quality time with Jane, whom she had not seen since the summer.

Jane would be arriving on December 13, so she had basically less than four weeks to hit the job market and head-hunter agencies pretty aggressively in order to try to land a new contract prior the holidays.

4

Lady

As Baberuth was starting to act up, she got the hint that it must be time for his walk around the field and, before putting her laptop on snooze mode, she decided to check her email quickly to see if she had had any responses to her job applications.

A new email was in her mailbox from Karl Klederman. A year ago, she had had an interview with Karl, who was the general manager of Data Hardware in Munich. She had not got the job at the time, as he had felt that her poor German could be an issue. However, as they had a good contact the first time around, she had, a few days earlier, dropped him a short note to let him know that she was on the hunt again and, should he hear of anything going around in the neighbourhood, she would appreciate him pinging her.

The email from Karl was short and to the point:

Lorie,

Would you be available for an interview this week Wednesday, Thursday, or Friday afternoon?

Regards.

All right, she thought. On that positive note, she put her laptop on snooze and went up to get ready for Baberuth's late afternoon walk.

The air was cold, crisp and dry, just the way Lorie loved it. She had always favoured mountain-type weather over the rainy, damp and cold of the seaside. Even during the hot season, she tended to avoid beaches, most probably due to the fact that she had grown up on the sea coast. Her memories of beach holidays were childhood ones of crispy sand sandwiches prepared by her grandmother. On that day, there was snow on the ground, which made her surroundings even nicer to her. The white coat spread over the countryside clashing with the rich green colour of the pine trees from the small forest gave her a feeling of total peace, as if there was absolutely nothing wrong with the world.

Once they got to the little turn off, Lorie hooked Baberuth on his lead again to finish the walk back to the house.

After they got back, she gave him his usual dinner of pasta and the best dog meat she could find. Baberuth was somewhat overweight, but, although she kept him on a lean meat diet, all the treats and biscuits were somewhat proving counterproductive to Baberuth's Weight Watcher's plan.

Whilst observing the solid beast moving his big mouth around his bowl as fast as he possibly could, she could not help herself from smiling, thinking how life must be simple when you are a dog. As she carried on watching the old boy, who obviously was enjoying his dinner greatly, she decided that she would go down to her computer and run a search for a housemate for Baberuth.

They say you should not choose your dog; your dog should choose you. Apparently that piece of wisdom extended itself to the cyber highways as, bingo, before she knew it, she was looking at the picture of a cute little lady dog with *huge* ears. Lorie was so excited by the picture of the pooch that she immediately dialled the number and made an appointment with the current owner so that the little lady and Baberuth could have a blind date together to evaluate if they could get on.

The appointment had been set two days later and she could not wait to find out if this little lady would be the right sister-come-girlfriend for Baberuth.

Lorie could not believe how fast all the blocks seemed to be falling in the right way like dominos, first with the email from Karl, then finding a new dog so quickly, but, despite the good fortune she felt suddenly blessed with, she was not ready to share any of the news with anyone until the deals were actually in the bag and that meant not until she had signed a new contract and Baberuth was enjoying his new housemate.

Baberuth and Lady seemed to be at ease with each other as Lorie and the owners were walking them around the town to assess if this alliance could work or not. Lorie was so happy to drive off with Lady on the front seat that she could not help but laugh at Baberuth sitting straight up on the backseat, staring at Lady, and then at Lorie, as if to ask: *why* does she get to ride on the front seat and I don't?. The journey home was very peaceful and Lady took to her new home like a fish to water.

* * *

November was drawing to a close and the snow was getting thicker on the ground, but, as the days were getting colder and shorter, the low winter sun gave the landscape a warm, clean atmosphere that Lorie simply found energising.

That evening, coming back from another relaxing walk around the field with her two dogs, she put some water on the cooker to boil for the doggy pasta and pressed speed dial on her phone, selecting her mother's number:

"Hi, Mum, how are you?"

"Oh, *hi*! Hang on; let me turn the TV down. How are you?" asked her mother.

"I am good, thanks. I guess I need to share that the family has just got bigger," said Lorie.

"Bigger? What do you mean by bigger?" asked her mum.

"Her name is Lady," replied Lorie.

"Another dog? Huh, why did you do that? Baberuth, sweet as he is, gives you enough work; why would you possibly want to add to it?"

Although Lorie's mother loved Baberuth, she was always very critical on how he made the house dirty all the time. Her constant site comments were very unwelcomed by Lorie, who saw well beyond the dog's hair everywhere and the constant dirty paws on her floors. In the best of times, Lorie would dismiss and ignore the jelly fish comments from her mother, but, in a moment of irritation, during one of her mother's visits, Lorie pointed out to her mother that, although Baberuth might well be the generator of extra house work, at least he was always happy to see her, never asked her for cash and never made bad remarks to her on her appearance or that she was working too much or that she was late to give him his dinner. Since that time, Lorie's mother had put her venomous comments on hold, but, obviously, the news of four extra paws in the house and more dog hairs to deal with got the better of Lorie's mother.

As she pushed back on her mother's remark, the old dame got curious about the new family member and started to ask Lorie some questions about Lady, which showed interest. As Lorie put the phone down, she felt happy about the outcome of the conversation and, deep down, knew that, once her mother had been introduced to Lady, she would be fine with the idea.

She kept herself busy each day, sending out job applications, and had set herself a personal target for each day; she needed to send a minimum of five applications, even for jobs that would not quite fit, but where she felt that the recruiting company in question might be interested in her profile and experience.

II
Merry Christmas

1

A Smiley for You

'MBenson has sent you a smiley,' the incoming email from e-connections said.

Hey, hey, let's see, she thought. Her approach to this Internet dating thing was not to solicit anyone, but to let people contact her, and she would take it from there.

MBenson was, according to his profile, an engineer, living in Munich, the same age as she was, and had quite a nice smile on his photo.

Here goes nothing, she thought as she pressed the 'smile back' icon.

After finishing her cup of coffee, she went back upstairs to get dressed and take Baberuth and Lady for their morning walk.

"Come on, Sleeping Beauty!" she told the old boy, who was spread across the bed waiting for her to be ready to go out.

After they got back from the walk, she jumped in the shower and, whilst enjoying the feeling of the warm water running down her back, she planned out her day. Being in control of her own time was alien to her. This was not a concept she was accustomed to as, whilst working, her time controlled her and every minute of the day was already spoken for before she even got out of bed.

She turned off the water, stepped out of the shower, put on her pink Nikky suit, which she tended to favour when she was at home, and went back to her office after making a short detour to the kitchen to pick up fresh coffee, then started to labour herself with job hunting.

As she logged onto the computer, she saw another email from econnection informing her that she had received a message from Chuck Davies.

Interesting, she thought. She looked at Chuck Davis' profile and smiled. Chuck Davis was also an engineer who was located in Munich and, funny enough, also worked in the petroleum industry, just like Mike Benson.

She read the short email and pressed the 'reply' button, thanking him for his message and asking him a few questions.

The phone rang.

"Hi, Lorie, it is Sophie."

Sophie was an old-time work colleague with whom she had worked in the UK. Sophie was actually the one who had pushed Lorie's CV on the CFO's desk of her last company.

"How are you doing? Did they give you a good package to leave?" Sophie asked.

"Hi, Sophie. I am doing okay; enjoying having a little bit of free time for a change," said Lorie.

"Well, I wish they would give me a package, too. I am so fed up with all their political bullshit. All I do is travel, but there is no satisfaction or joy here anymore."

"I can understand that, Sophie; us working girls, we just seem to be giving our blood and life away for no return, really. Anyway, with my mother and Jane coming over for Christmas, I want to try to get a contract before Christmas. It is very aggressive, but, nevertheless, there seem to be some prospects out there, so we shall see."

"Let me know how you are getting on," said Sophie. "I

need to go and catch my flight now, but I will give you a call in the next few days."

"Travel safely. I will let you know if anything happens on my side."

Lorie spent the remainder of the morning going through the Internet job portals, sending a few CVs out, and making calls to job hunters.

Having secured an appointment with Karl Klederman, she felt hopeful that this could be just what she needed to guarantee herself a pay cheque at least for the coming year. 2009 had been a very tough year for her, and she was hoping that, by being back in Munich and with a new job, 2010 would be somewhat a little bit less stressful. Keeping that thought in mind, she decided to go out for the afternoon, take a little gym time, pick up food for her, Baberuth and Lady, and stop by the DVD rental shop to pick up a movie for the evening.

The phone rang.

"Hi, it's Maggie."

Maggie was probably the only friend she was able to spend quality time with. Like Lorie, Maggie was in her forties and single. Maggie had worked for over three years for Lorie as her assistant when Lorie was still with INSPECT Technology. After Lorie got made redundant due the merger, Maggie and Lorie kept in touch and regularly got together over tea and cake for a catch up.

"Hi, Maggie, hang on; let me put the phone down for a sec; I need to put the pasta on for Baberuth." After doing so, she returned to the call. "Okay, done; how are you doing, Maggie? Have they fired you yet?"

Maggie laughed sarcastically. "No, but I wish they would. But hey, I am not going on my own, although Clive is doing everything he can to push me out."

"Good on you, girl. You dig your heels in and wait until they get tired and come to you with a cheque."

"Lorie, it is not fun here anymore. These people are so nasty, but I just do what I need to do and go home. How are things with you?"

"Okay, I guess. I am trying to enjoy my free time a little bit, but, at the same time, I find it hard to relax, as I need to get a new job before Christmas."

"Have you got anything yet?" asked Maggie.

"Maybe; not sure; I will tell you more in a couple of days"

"I am curious now, how on earth did you get a prospect so quickly?"

"Can't tell you. Maggie, I need to go now, but I will call you in a couple of days," Lorie replied to her friend.

"Can't wait! Have a good evening," Maggie said.

"Thanks, you too," said Lorie, ending the conversation.

Lorie put the phone down right on time to drain the doggy pasta, served Baberuth and Lady a generous portion each, and proceeded with putting her dinner on a tray.

She fed the DVD player the disk, switched on the film and enjoyed her food in a very relaxed manner.

* * *

The next day, Lorie fell out of bed feeling quite happy and upbeat at the thought of her meeting with Karl Kledermann.

She put on her best suit, printed out the address for Data Hardware and, after checking herself out in the hallway mirror, walked out the door.

It took her fifty minutes to get to the company, which she thought was okay as far as commuting time was concerned.

"Good morning, Lorie. Thank you for coming at such short notice," said Karl.

"Pleasure is all mine. How can I be of assistance?"

Karl explained to Lorie that the person they had opted

for over her six months ago was not quite working out and, as such, Karl was waiting for him to come back from holiday to discuss a possible separation. They talked for over an hour and Karl told Lorie that he would be in touch in the next week or so.

As she left the building and walked towards her car, she was very relaxed and confident that the search for her next pay cheque might well be over.

2

A Turkey and a Job

The mood in the house was jolly and somewhat festive as the three ladies were planning their Christmas celebration. Lorie needed to go to the nearby town to pick up her mother's Christmas present. That year, Lorie finally had her wish come true by getting a picture of Jane, herself and the two dogs made by a professional photographer.

Pulling out of a her driveway, she saw that she was out of petrol and drove first to the next petrol station to tank up. As she pulled the car next to the pump, someone tapped on her window. A tall man was standing next to her car shouting at her in German. She came out of the car to see what it was all about. The man pointed at the back of her vehicle. She walked around, looked down and saw that, for the last ten kilometres or so, she had been dragging an old, broken set of Christmas tree lights that had been caught in her wheel as she had pulled out of her garage. The man was standing spitting out verbal arrows at her, which she did not quite understand, but it was clear by his tone that he was by no mean a happy camper.

As she was looking at the light and observing the man's reaction, she started to laugh. She looked at the man and, with a big smile, said to him in broken German, "Well, it is Christmas, after all! Happy Christmas to you.

Then she carried on fuelling up her car.

The man stood there for a good couple of minutes staring at her in disbelief, and eventually walked away in a grump. That made Lorie laugh even more, as she said out loud to herself that people should lighten up.

Once she got home, she carefully handed over the present to Jane for her to wrap up and put under the tree, and the phone rang.

"Hi, Lorie, this is Karl."

Karl told Lorie that he would be, this very day, sending her a contract offer to her email address, and that he would appreciate it if she could review it and give him an answer by the end of the following week.

Lorie felt overjoyed as, yes, the search had ended and, against all odds, she had put a new work contract on the table next to her Christmas turkey.

Life was good, and this was bound to be the Christmas she had hoped to give to her mother and her daughter.

The three ladies spent the afternoon in the nearby town picking up the last stoking fillers and the remaining bits and pieces for their celebration dinner. It was the end of the afternoon, by the time they returned back to the house. They got themselves busy preparing their Christmas Eve dinner. Everyone was very jolly. The three of them put on their best dresses before sitting at the table and, once all settled ready to enjoy their feast, they raised their glasses to what had been a very nice and simple, yet truly enjoyable day.

"I would like to make an announcement," said Lorie as she was holding up her glass filled with iced tea.

"An announcement?" echoed her mother quizzically.

"Well, the call I received this morning was about a new contract with a company in Munich."

"Oh my, sweet Jesus!" exclaimed her mother.

Lorie had done a great job in disguising the fact that she,

in reality, had been out of a job for the past four weeks, so, as she pursued sharing her good fortune with her mother and daughter, she felt a tremendous amount of relief, peacefulness and, most of all, she felt full of hope that 2010 would be the year when she would finally bring her life back together.

Following their dinners, the three ladies gathered around the tree and exchanged their presents. Jane received quite a lot of money, some clothes and various cosmetic items. Mother received a shawl, a music CD from Jane and the family portrait, which she totally adored and for which she had a hard time containing her tears. Lorie received a piece of jewellery, some money, a new telephone set, as hers was so old that the numbers could no longer be seen on the screen, and a new handbag.

Baberuth and Lilly both received a cuddly toy and a big bone as a treat.

It was a truly one of the best Christmases Lorie could remember in many years and she had a feel-good sensation running through her, a sensation of serenity and being at peace with the world. She had not felt like that for a very long time.

* * *

The following morning was busy and exciting. Lorie had rolled out of bed at 6 a.m. to prepare the traditional turkey lunch. Since they had arrived in Germany, each Christmas they would get a fresh turkey from the nearby farm and end up living off it until well into the New Year, as the beast did not come in small sizes. For the two previous years, the farmer had agreed to provide Lorie with just half a turkey, as he appreciated the fact that, since Lorie only had her mother and daughter over, a full one would be somewhat of an overkill.

Whilst Lori stayed in the kitchen under the watchful eyes of her two four-legged kitchen assistants, she suddenly remembered that maybe she should look at her emails, which she had not done for a couple of days. After carefully feeding the turkey to the oven, she went down to her office and booted up her laptop.

She saw the contract that Karl had sent to her, read it through and replied to him that everything was fine and that she would be putting the signed copy in the post to him during the following week. Her starting date had been set for January 15 and, for her, that was perfect, as it would give her time to re-organise the dogs' sitting schedule with her neighbour and finish her house projects, which she had started prior to the holidays.

III

Happy Valentine's

1

Howdy, Partner

Lorie had been so busy getting back into a day-to-day work routine again and settling into her newfound job since she had resumed work life on January 15 that she had forgotten about econnections until she saw the last message that Chuck Davies had written to her, and decided to answer it.

From:Dahlfi65@xxxxxx
To: cdavies74@xxxxxx
Subject: econnections
Date: Tuesday, February 2. 2010: 08:43

Howdy, Partner,

Just saw your message. So sorry for the late note. Anyway, I initially replied on the econnections mailbox, so have a look.
Tell me, are you sure you have the right girl? I have my charms, but beauty, you are pushing the envelop a little, but keep going; I like it and I like myself just fine.
   ... And so that you remember, I have again attached my photo.
Hope to hear from you very soon.

Take care,
Lorie

Judging by the email sitting in her mail box the next day, the man in question had not forgotten about econnections, or her, for that matter. She read the email in amusement:

From: cdavies74@xxxxxx
To: Dahlfi65@xxxxxx
Subject: econnections.
Date: Tuesday. February 2. 2010: 15:43

Late response! But it's better late than never, you know
smile. I don't go on econnections anymore, so I think it's
better to write to you here; just to let you know, I am not in
Germany; a friend from Germany helped me open this
profile. I am in my country now (USA, Texas).
   They say beauty is in the eye of the beholder and, in our
own case, I believe I am the beholder, so I say you are
beautiful. I would love to know if you will give me a chance. I
don't have a woman. I am divorced, so I live alone now and
my ex got custody of the kids.
Thanks for the beautiful picture, Lorie. Hope to hear from you
soon.

Kisses to you,
Chuck

How about that, she thought. Texas, *hello*! *This guy has some nerve posting a profile on a German website. Typical!* It was yet again more evidence that her life would never be straight forward and that, in all realms of it, she would have to jump through hoops of fire to get what she wanted. She could easily accept that fact when it came to professional challenges, but, in relationships, she would not have entertained that idea whatsoever. It was what it was, and, without giving it a second thought, she pressed the reply button.

From:Dahlfi65@xxxxxx
To Cdavis74@xxxxxx
Subject::econnections
Date:Tuesday February 2, 2010 17:31

Oh, so now he lets the horses out of the barn!

Texas! That's like zillions of kilometres away (I know; I have been there).

So, what are you exactly hoping for, being in Texas and sweet talking some girl in Bavaria? (Although, I do understand that, because of your boys.)

Having said that, and having read your nice emails and seen the great pictures, I would not mind finding out more about you, too. I do not have a man, either, but I do not live alone. I have two great dogs, and I have also been gifted with a beautiful daughter who is currently studying at uni in the UK... and, by the way, I am not German, either...

So what's your plan now, big guy?

Lorie

2

Moving to Germany

For the following days, Lorie concentrated fully on her new job, trying to connect with her new colleagues and, first and foremost, her team. Her team would be a problem for her. The challenge she was facing with the very small group went far beyond the language difficulty, which was clear, but nevertheless, understood by her boss.

Lorie had relocated to Germany with her late husband and daughter ten years prior, following a big centralisation exercise that had been carried out by Inspect, her company at the time.

She could never forget that time. Back then, they lived in a small village outside of Slough, Berkshire. Her and her husband worked for the same company and, as they had both finally achieved stability in their jobs following twelve years of moving around a lot, they had found themselves in a position to purchase a small starter home, which was newly built. They also managed to enrol Jane in a private Christian school, which was two minutes away from their office, so, all in all, life had settled and had been going well.

For the second year running, they took their two-weeks yearly family holiday over Easter, and went back to Florida, bringing Mother along for the ride. Lorie's father had passed away the previous November, and she and her husband had thought it would be good for the old dame to do something a little different. Furthermore, Lorie was not happy going so far away, knowing her mother would find it hard to cope with them being out of pocket, so to speak.

In order to fit Mother on the trip, which had already been booked well before her dad's death, Lorie had to organise for them to fly separately. Her husband, John, and Jane, flew together through Atlanta, whilst Lorie and Mother took the Miami route.

Upon their return, when Lorie walked through the front door on that particular Easter Monday, Mother in tow, her husband literally pounced on her, telling her that she should call Mike, her boss, immediately and, with barely taking in air to breathe, told her that he had found over twenty messages on the answering machine instructing them to make contact as soon as they got back regardless of whether it was day or night.

Without even taking her jacket off, Lorie dialled Mike's home number. The conversation was short and to the point. The company was moving all back-office functions in Munich, and the European board wanted Lorie and her husband to relocate to Munich to set up the departments. Lorie was told that the moving was set for July, which left them basically just a little over than three months to move jobs, house, kid, etcetera… The news came down like a rock on the group and they spent the whole day discussing this new prospect.

After moving to Germany, Lorie and her husband never looked back on making that move as, despite the language barrier, they fell in love with their newfound surroundings and its country feeling. Carrier-wise, the move had been more than beneficial for Lorie and John

Work and life ran pretty smoothly for them, and Jane, despite her constant winging and moaning, seemed to have settled really well at the international school in the village.

Thanks to the incredible support that Lorie received from the firm after her husband had tragically died, Lorie had managed by applying a lot of financial juggling, to keep Jane at the school, and even made the move of buying the house they were living in so that her daughter would get a sense of security.

As life felt somewhat stable, her company was eventually acquired. Every acquisition was followed up with a merger, and it was clear from the very start of this merger that she, for sure, was not part of the go-forward team. This did not worry her at the time, as, based on what she saw from the acquiring company, it was transparent to her that she could never fit in their philosophy. Eventually, on a sunny Monday, she was told boldly and without any warning by the VP of human resources, over pizza and pasta at the little Italian corner restaurant, that they wanted to discuss a separation agreement. That stone in the soup was dropped sheepishly between talking about kids, mothers and the weather.

This came as no surprise to her; however, she felt disgusted by the approach and her reaction to the bullet was to burst out laughing, as she could not help but find it extremely amusing that her boss had gone through all the trouble of putting Peter on a plane to Munich to fire her, as he obviously did not have the balls to do it himself. He never struck her as having any balls, anyway, so no surprise there.

Peter got seriously thrown out by her reaction. Knowing her strong character, he had obviously decided to take her out to a public place to avoid any emotional outburst or drama, but what he had failed to anticipate was her actually bursting out laughing. His face was quite a picture and she had told herself many times afterwards that she should have picked up his plate of spaghetti Bolognese and dropped it on his head. Boy, that would have made quite a hot topic of conversation in the office for the afternoon, considering the fact that half the company ate at the little Italian restaurant, and that day was no different to any other, as the place was packed with Inspect employees. Since that day, she would always relate to the incident as the day she got fired like Jerry McGuire.

Lorie dutifully worked her three months' notice, although she only went there to assume presence, as she obviously had no direct responsibilities anymore. She used that time to put her CV together and slowly hand over to her assistant the various bits and pieces she had on her desk.

On her first day as a free woman, as she put it, she looked around her house, breathed deeply and tried to put a strategy together on how she was going to handle the future. However, first and foremost, she was going to take the whole summer off, as she had not had a break, known as holidays, for a very long time. Inspect gave her a good package, so she was going to take her time and treat herself. Autumn would be there soon enough, and she would then attack the job market very aggressively.

Moving around her house, picking things up, she realised that she should go and get some food. It hit her there and then: car. She no longer had a car, as she had had to give back the company BMW, and then it slowly cascaded down through her mind: no car, no Internet, as the company had been paying for it; luckily enough, she had got a private mobile phone few months ago, but she had completely missed out on the car and Internet.

Okay, well, never mind. She grabbed Baberuth's leash who was seven at the time and decided to walk to the village, which was only two and a half kilometres away. The fresh air would do her good and she had all the time in the world for a change.

Lorie's summer did not quite work out as she had

planned, as, very shortly after her leaving the company, she ended up in hospital being diagnosed with multiple infections. It was put down to the change of pace in her life and, as her body relaxed, her immune system ended up collapsing, too. Lorie spent the whole summer in and out of hospital and, with two surgeries in the bag, her so-wanted and deserved holiday came quickly to a close, as she needed to secure a job pretty quickly.

The search was difficult as, although she had a wealth of experience, the doors were being shut in her face on the basis that she did not speak good enough German. Lorie felt extremely embarrassed by the fact that, despite having been in Germany for so many years, her language abilities had barely taken off the ground. All those years, she had completely lived in a closed and safe bubble, only rubbing shoulders with expatriates like herself from all geographies, and English was what linked them together. She, of course, had picked up some basic speaking skills along the way, if pointing at what you want at the supermarket counter can be counted as a communication skill.

The years had gone by and she was still pointing at the sausages at the supermarket. It had become very much her lifestyle and she had no issues with it, as it served the purpose perfectly.

Eventually, she got a lead from Sophie that PC Anywhere was looking for someone in finance, and Sophie had pushed Lorie's CV down the CFO's throat. After that, the process was quick and, before she knew it, Lori was back on the job working as an international cash manager. Although the environment was more German, English was still her main communication engine, as she worked internationally.

3

The Hell Team

After leaving PC Anywhere, she had, through push and shove, picked up more of the language, but, in a professional capacity, her pigeon German did not quite cut it. Klaus had known that fact, but she had something else to offer, and he had made the decision to take the chance and see how things would work out.

When Lori had attended a meeting prior to her starting, to meet with her new team, she had felt an icy draft on her shoulders. She knew then that she would have to put a lot of effort into get these guys on board.

Her intuition got more and more confirmed as true, each day. The iron curtain that had obviously been raised between them and her got thicker and thicker, making her wonder how she was going to get around that one. This group was not going to play ball, so she decided, in the first instance, not to act as a bull in a China shop, and canned their sorry backsides one after the other, which, in hindsight, would have been the right decision, but she had opted at the time for the other option, which was to sit back instead and give them the chance to warm up to her.

4

Engineer! Say What?

After coming home from work that Friday, Lori picked up
her phone to call Maggie, in order to make arrangements to
meet up the following Sunday. A few years ago, Lorie had
taken Maggie to see the Holiday on Ice show for her
birthday. When Lorie was a little girl, her parents took her
every year to see the Ice review in her home town. As she
made her life as an adult, she never had the chance to go
again until that year. She always wanted to and thought it
would be a nice idea as a birthday present for Maggie. The
previous two years, she had not had the opportunity to do
so, as she was commuting constantly for her job, so she
made a point not to miss the opportunity that year. She
viewed it as a chance to kill two birds with the one stone.
On one hand, it would be like re-connecting with her
childhood, which felt very much like another lifetime for her
and, on the other hand, it would be her own way to show
Maggie how much she appreciated her ongoing friendship.

"Hi, Maggie, it's Lorie. I am calling to find out how we
should meet on Sunday?"

"I think it is best if we meet in front of the arena thirty
minutes before the show. Does this work for you?"

"Okay, perfect! And afterwards we can go for coffee
and cake, and I will drive you home."

"Good. I will see you there."

"Thanks, Lorie, I am really looking forward to this."

"Me too, Maggie."

She put the phone down and, after going through her normal evening routines of feeding the dogs and changing from her office attire to her leisure clothes, she went down to her office and booted up her computer.

She had received a message from Curtis Wells. His first message was short and sweet, just thanking her for her note.

How about that, she thought. She had noticed him on the econnection website and had found him quite cute, but she had kept to her approach not to ping anyone, and was quite excited that he had, a few days earlier, made the first step by sending her a one-liner, 'hi, how are you doing' note.

She saw also that there was a message from Chuck Davies. She was started to feel irritated by this man, who was getting demanding, and that email got even more on her nerves.

From: cdavies74@xxxxxx
To: Dahlfi65@xxxxxx
Subject: econnections
Date: Saturday, February 13, 2010 17:31

Hello, Lorie,

How are you doing? Been two days now and I didn't hear anything from you; is everything all right with you? If your number will go through, I will call you when I get home in thirty minutes, okay.

Kisses to you,
Chuck.

She decided to let him stew a little more, switched off her laptop and went to bed.

After dinner, she finished watching her weekly movie and, as she did not feel tired, she decided to go down to her laptop to answer Curtis using her proper email, as, for some reason, she was comfortable with him. In his most recent reply to her, he had thanked her for replying, which she had appreciated very much, as it gave her the sense that he had good manners and etiquette.

From: Lorie.finnighan@xxxxxx
To: curtiswells62@xxxxxx
Subject: Happy Valentines.
Date: Saturday, February 13, 2010.10:52pm.

Hi, Curtis,

I feel very flattered that you have taken the time to write to me. I love your English! Trust me, you don't want to suffer my German... Grosse Baustelle (construction site) and very painful.

Anyhoo, I would be happy to find out more about you... I love your smile, by the way... Just in case, you don't remember which one of the one hundred women you wrote to, I have included my picture.

Yes, I have been getting quite a lot of attention, but only the wrong kind, so far.

Well, I don't know you, but let me wish you a very happy Valentine's Day, anyway.

Kindest regards,
Lorie.

The following morning, as she routinely grabbed her first coffee, she went down to her office to check her email, she was amazed to find another message from Curtis.

From: curtiswells62@xxxxxx
To: loriefinnighan@xxxxx
Subject: Happy Valentines
Date: Saturday, February 13, 2010 11:48 p.m.

Hello, Laurie,

Thanks for the message; it was really good to read from you, and I also hardly get messages from a lot of women, so I was sure going to be able to know you were the one writing, but thanks anyway for the picture. It was nice and you do have a lovely smile. Just thought I give you a message about me... What can I tell you about me?

Well... I was married for thirteen years, but now I am divorced since September 5; this woman I have known since college, but we never did expect something serious I fell in love, we started having problems when she was sleeping with another man, and she requested a divorce after she had been cheating on me; we both lived in Ireland... I moved to Irvine, California, in the US, with my son. Lived here since February 2006, and I have full custody of my six-year-old old son. It was last year November that I decided to move to Germany, so we can settle in Europe, so I am still learning a lot about Berglern. I live there with my son and I love it here. I'm forty-seven and I work for a company that designs tractor cooling systems, am 6'0", and have dark brown hair and brown eyes, but I haven't been happy, right now. I do travel a lot; actually, travelling on business trips was kinda fun, and I have been to some wonderful cities in Europe and a dozen other old cities, and some parts of South America, too, but, without someone special to share it all with, it just wasn't the same kind of experience it could have been. I am actually in West Africa since February 5, for a business dealing, and maybe when we converse more I will let you know what business I am doing here.... I have really met a lot of women ... but I noticed most of them are liars and some are not ready to be a good wife, so I just had to let it go not until a friend of mine told me about this site and I decided to give it a trial;

maybe I can find my woman here. I really like what I saw on your profile. I am very truthful and detest liars. I have noticed that the reason that so many men and women don't have success with having relationships is that they simply are so concerned with finding someone for their own personal gain instead of examining what they have to offer a relationship. When I was younger, I wanted to find Mrs. Right. I was so caught up in what I wanted her to be for me that I neglected to focus also on what I had to offer. That is as important in a relationships' success as finding what you want. I have learnt the hard way that the Mrs. Rights involved also had a right to find what was going to be of benefit to them. I think part of the reason that we fail so miserably at relationships is that we think that we have so much to offer when the reality is that we were doing more taking than offering and, when the relationship fails, we come up with this 'she likes bad boys', 'she wants money' or 'he is too shallow' – this, that or the other. If you put yourself on the market and you truly want real love, you must have some real love of your own to offer. If you do not, then why should you have something that you don't have to offer? My dad was Baptist and mom Jewish, and, by Jewish law, I am a Jew, as well, but not a very practicing one, though I sometimes celebrated their holidays with my mom when they were alive. I guess I just try to fit into both, which is nice, so having a woman with any religion won't be a problem for me. I must let you know that I am prepared to look for that right person whom I will be able to share love with no matter where she is. I am very much open to and I understand that long-distance relationships can be hard, though I haven't tried it, but I wouldn't let distance or age difference deter me from meeting that right person, 'cos I believe age is just a number; what matters is that our hearts yearn for each other.

Wow! I already wrote a whole novel… lol. Anyway, do you have other instant messenger services like Yahoo or MSN that we can both connect on, as I would like to know more about you, and that is the easiest and fastest means of communication for me.

Have a good one, and Happy Valentine's Day.

Curtis.

Holy smoke, she thought. *This guy sure has a lot on his mind.* However, she did find his email interesting and would get back to him at some stage.

She went up and, keeping to her usual ways, got kitted up to brace the morning's snowy, cold weather with her two faithful companions. Whilst she was going around the field keeping watchful eyes on Lady and Baberuth, who seemed to be getting down to business leaving evidences of their passage along the way, she was trying to think what she should answer to Curtis. He sure had put some work and thought into that email, but that was a lot of information for her to digest at such an early stage of their newfound online connection.

As they walked back into the house, Lorie took off her boots and her jacket, refilled her previously discarded cup with fresh coffee, and went down to her office to answer Curtis.

From:loriefinnighan@xxxxxx
To:curtiswells62@xxxxxx
Subject:Happy Valentines.
Date:Sunday February 14th, 2010 08:52 am

A very good, good morning from snowy Bavaria to you, Curtis!
That was quite a long message, but I do appreciate you taking the time to write back. Frankly, I am quite fed up myself and I was about to completely drop this Internet dating solution until I saw your message. Point is that I had open the lines of communication with four other gentlemen, 'but, one by one, shut them down, and I just sent the last cowboy back on his horse. I was always sceptical about this Internet dating

thing. I know it has been very successful in some cases and with people I know, even, but, for me, I always felt it was somewhat unnatural, too much like shopping on eBay for a relationship (yuk).

Having said that and, if I was to reflect on my current life set up, my best chance to meet someone new would seem to be by queuing up at the supermarket meat counter on Saturday mornings (although that could be fun... hmm, need to pay more attention when I go grocery shopping again next Saturday).

So, since you were forthcoming enough with your own background and the reason why you are single (a good-looking guy like you; it is hard to believe), maybe I should return the favour.

Well, I am forty-four and a half. I would like to say that the reason for my 'single-hood' state is due to a marriage gone bad, but my husband of sixteen years was the extreme type and decided to die suddenly on me of an aneurism on a sunny Sunday afternoon six years ago. That's life! Since then, I have been focussing on my daughter and my job, which has left me very little time for anything else, let alone dating. However, the sheer thought of growing old and never having someone special again in my life is just freaking me out, so, against my better judgment, I decided to post a profile on the Internet and see what would happen next. Now, to go back to the top of this message, all I have seen so far has simply been disheartening and aggravating, not to say the least.

I have a nineteen-year-old daughter who is currently studying at Glasgow University in the UK. She is a great kid and I am her biggest fan and admirer.

From the job spec, well, I am working as a finance manager for a US software reseller. I like my job very much, but there has to be more to life than that.

Like having a nice companion to do fun stuff with and share the experiences or simply the day's events is something that I would love to have, so I keep open minded.

I do have messenger, but on MSN, not on Yahoo, but you are right; this is a good and efficient way to communicate, so, if we keep on exchanging messages, we can do something about getting on the same platform.

And please, just to be sure, do you really live in the neighbourhood? The reason I am asking this is that the last three amigos had Munich on their profiles, but eventually it turned out that one was living in Virginia and just coming to Germany from time to time for work, the second one was living in Florida, but was kind of thinking of relocating to Munich for business (sorry, honey, first you relocate, and then we can talk), and last, but not least, the last one is actually living in Dallas, TX, has never been to Germany, and seemed to think that I would have no issue relocating to TX, just like that! So, I hope you appreciate my position here. For me, in order to build a connection, I need to have the face to face, and even it is not each day every day due to professional or private reasons, at least be able to meet up at from time to time; well, I hope you know what I am trying to say. I need to have the physical connection as much as the emotional one... So that you know...

Okay, on that novel of mine, I will leave you in peace and wish you a very good day in Africa or wherever you might be today.

Kindest regards,
Lorie.

PS: I forgot to mention that I was French.

After shutting down her computer, she proceeded with her morning plan and kept checking the time so that she would not be late to meet up with Maggie. Despite her best efforts, she did not quite make it on time due to parking challenges that led to her having to park outside the sport complex and walk around the arena for thirty minutes, with Maggie on her mobile phone trying to guide her in the right direction and failing miserably in the process.

"Did you like the show?" Lorie asked Maggie

"Yes, I really enjoyed it. It is a great way to spend a

Sunday afternoon. Thank you so much; let me treat you to coffee and cake."

"Absolutely!"

The two women headed back to the car, and chit chatted about work and other general life topics. After walking around Munich Main Street for a short while, they settled on a teahouse and placed their order.

"So, said Maggie, what has been happening with those guys you told me about the other day?"

"Ah, my Internet boyfriends, you mean?" asked Lorie, laughing.

"Well, go on; I am very curious."

"I am telling you, Maggie, this is turning to be quite an interesting past time," said Lorie. "So far, I have been in contact with four. You really need to hear this…

"The first one, Mike Benson, well, this guy is an engineer for a petroleum company, and currently lives in New England, travels a lot, and told me that he would contact me when he was back in Munich. Except that I have not heard from him since just before Christmas.

"The second one, Mathew Osmond. Another oil engineer, would you believe, who happens to live in Florida, but is currently in Africa. That one, Maggie, did not last long with me as, one night during one of our messenger chats, he tried to sell me a tear jerker story about a day there had been an accident on one of the oil platform where some of his local guys were working and two of them died. One of them was apparently a father with twins. At first, I told him that I was sorry to hear that and that it must be quite difficult for him. But then he asked me if I would make a donation for the families. I kind of questioned him on his insurance status, and he told me that his insurance did not cover such accidents and that he needed to give these guys money to avoid a law suit, and that I should send the donation through Western Union."

"You did not, I hope," said Maggie.

"Of course not; instead, I told him that I had issues with the fact that he used underpaid, under-trained local labour without having taken the proper insurances to protect these very people. So that was that; never heard from him again. The third one, Chuck Davies! Now that one is a piece of work. He lives in Texas and has six boys, would you believe, but, surprise, surprise, he is also an oil engineer who is trying to set up his own business in Ethanol distribution."

"What's that?" asked Maggie.

"Apparently, Ethanol is the more environmental friendly version of gasoline, and is mainly used for big industrial vehicles and farming vehicles. According to him, there is a lot of money to be made as the production of Ethanol as well as Ethanol equipment is only in its infancy, and there are only a few distributors at the moment."

"Never heard of it," said Maggie.

"Neither had I, until now," said Lorie. "Now what is funny there is that the only reason I had actually answered those guys is that they had put their location as Munich, but, as he turned out, they were all, in fact, living in the US. That is so bizarre. When I questioned them on that, they all said that apparently the women in Europe are more family orientated than in the US and that they also would like to extend their businesses to Europe.

"Anyhow, then comes along Franklin. Now, Franklin is not an engineer... How refreshing!" said Lorie, laughing. "Maggie, frankly, is rich. It turns out, or so he says that, he sells luxury yachts to the rich people and the who is who of this world. So, Franklin was quite interesting to start with, except that, my goodness, this man has serious issues."

"What do you mean issues?" asked Maggie.

"Emotional, capital 'e', Maggie! A real drama queen on email; a desperado of the first grade. I basically had to tell him to buzz off, as he kept sending me these long, emotionally loaded emails, and what really put me off was that he was using his adopted son, Sasha, to try to get to me. Boy, that really rubbed me the wrong way."

"Well, I guess I would have done the same thing."

"The funny part was that, despite me telling him that I thought he was way too emotional for me, he just kept on sending me emails and wanted to surprise me for Valentine's Day!"

"Oh, dear. What did you do?"

"I had to be a little hard on him and I basically told him that I did not want him to surprise me for Valentine's, as I was sorry to tell him that I had, in fact, taken interest in someone else." Curtis Wells was on her mind as she was sharing this with her friend.

"How did he react?"

"He did not. I never heard from him again. So, Goodbye, Franklin. But now, a new one has joined my fan club last night. His name is Curtis Wells, but why am I surprised; he is an engineer, as well, and he also is trying to set up his own Ethanol retailing venture, except that he wants to sell the equipment, not the liquid itself; as far as I understand, anyway."

"Don't tell me, he also lives in the US."

"Well, not anymore. He had told me that he had relocated with his six-year-old son, Joshua, to Munich – Bertglern, to be precise – back in November, but they were currently in Lagos, as he was in the process of buying equipment to ship back to the US."

"So that is quite funny, really, as the three guys I am currently actively communicating with right now happen to be in Nigeria for the same reason."

"Don't you think it is a little strange?"

"Yes, I do, actually, but it is quite fun, really, so I will see how this is going to develop."

After moving the conversation to other topics, the two women finally decided to leave, as it was getting late in the day. Lorie dropped Maggie back at her apartment and drove home.

As she got back home, she checked her emails and found a message from Jane, who was bitterly complaining about her job at McDonald's and wanted to quit. Lorie never liked the idea of Jane having to work to get extra cash, but she was not in the position at the time to provide Jane with all the financial support she needed. As she answered her daughter, she was trying to think of what she could do to help her out.

She also found a message from Chuck Davies, who was complaining again that she had not written to him and that she had obviously forgotten about his birthday, and even he went on by demanding that she call him. *That guy has got some nerve,* she thought, and, completely irritated, answered him:

From: Dahli65@xxxxxx
To: cdavies74@xxxxxx
Re: econnections
Date: February 14.2010 19:08

First and foremost, happy birthday!
One should be careful about jumping to the wrong conclusions. No, I had not forgotten your birthday and I find it quite fresh from you that you seem to demand that I call you— what are you, ten years old?
If you feel that I am not giving you enough attention (let alone the fact that I spent over an hour on the phone to you in the middle of the night), well, that's your problem, not mine. I start my day at 5:30 a.m. and get home at 8 p.m. five days a week; whenever I write a message to you, it is because I really want to do it not because I feel obliged to so. I have been quite clear that I will not be pushed or put under

pressure. I have also been clear that the distance was an issue for me, but I was in no rush and, since I like you, which I do, I was not going to shut you down for that reason (despite the fact that you had put Munich as a location on your profile, which was not honest, was it now).

I am happy that you are enjoying our communications, because I am, too, but sorry to say that you are not on my mind 24/7. That connection is not there for me; not yet, anyway.

So relax and take it easy. I do appreciate a man being protective, but possessive and controlling is a definite no-go with me.

This might come across as a hard message, but, since honesty is one of your big points, well, I have no issues being honest with you, even if I feel sorry about the timing being your birthday and all.

Get this and get this right: I will not be pushed, forced nor have expectations put on me. You cannot force feelings overnight, Chuck. It is something that grows with time.

Just be careful how you go forward with this; that's all I can say.

L.

There! Take that, partner! That should set you straight, cowboy, she thought.

As she pressed the 'sent' button, she saw an email coming from Curtis Wells.

From:curtiswells62@xxxxxx
To:loriefinnighan@xxxxxx
Subject:Re: Happy Valentines
Date Sunday February 14th, 2010 – 19:30 pm

Hello, Laurie,

Thanks for the message… It is really nice to read from you. I must say I was quite expecting a long email from you after the one I sent to you.

I am sure that you can add my Yahoo messenger with your MSN name.

I will be looking forward to hearing from you later.

I must say that I really liked what I read about you.

You sure have got my interest there and I would like to get to know more about you. I guess I will just try to add you so we can see if we can accept each other online through our respective messengers, and we will continue communication from there.

Hope to hear from you soon.

Cheers,
Curtis.

"And I guess you will hear from me soon," she said.

As her day drew to a close, she made her way to bed feeling quite good about Curtis' email whilst, at the same time, not quite sure how she would handle Chuck Davies, as he was becoming more demanding and controlling through his emails, let alone her receiving calls in the middle of the night, which she was finding harder to bear.

At that point, and with her being busy again, professionally speaking, she decided that she would not open the doors to any other potential romantic partnership candidate and would just keep casually communicating with Curtis whilst observing how Chuck was going to react to her more direct, to-the-point email.

Her week started pretty much normally and she found herself staying later and later in the office, trying to get her head around her new environment and going absolutely nowhere fast with getting her team to be little more forthcoming with her. She told herself that she needed to be patient, as her boss had been open enough with her to explain that the crew in question were going through their third leadership change in less than eighteen months. Armed with that knowledge, she tried to put herself in their shoes and could understand that they were not going to make it easy for her as, in their views, she would probably come and go just like the others, so why bother changing the work routine to which they had got accustomed to and felt comfortable with?

5

Ethanol, Gold Rush

The following morning was very calm and, as her crew had decided to walk down to the cafeteria for their break, she granted herself a break and checked her emails.

Chuck Davies… *Well, well, he is definitely not dropping the ball, that one,* she thought.

From: Cdavies74@xxxxxx
To: Dahlfi65@xxxxxx
Subject:econnections
Date:Tuesday, February 16, 2010 16:57pm

Hello, L,

Quite early here; it's 4:11 a.m. and, 'cos I am travelling today, I have to get all in place and leave to the airport early this morning. Dallas-Fort Worth International Airport (DFW/KDFW) is where I fly from. This airport is in Dallas/Ft. Worth, Texas, and is a hundred and thirty-one miles from the centre of Kilgore, so I will need to leave home early. I hope I will be able to write to you when I get there. So, what are your plans for this week?

Have a wonderful week.
Chuck.

Chuck had informed her that he would be going to West Africa for his ethanol business. She found that quite amusing, as Curtis had also told her that he was currently in Africa for his Ethanol business. This Ethanol craze started to turn into somewhat a gold rush in her mind. After reading the note, she closed her email and resumed her work.

The next day, she got another email from Chuck:

From:Cdavies74@xxxxxx
To: Dahlfi65@xxxxxxxx
Re:econnections
Date:Wednesday, February 17th, 2010 06:26pm

Hello, L,

Am sorry I didn't get to write to you yesterday; am in Nigeria already, and today was very busy for me, because I went to the stores from which I will be buying the cocoa beans, and I did some negotiation and all, but right now am back in the hotel where I lodge. Our conclusion is that a bag will cost some certain amount, and each bag will weigh a hundred and ninety pounds. I would love to hear your voice if you can call me; it's too expensive to call outside this country; I called my kids already. Anyways, the number to reach me on is +234XXXXXXX. Will be looking forward to hearing from you.

Chuck.

"You sure wrote to me yesterday," she said outloud.
   Boy, this guy has guts asking me to call him in Nigeria. He obviously missed out the part in one of her emails about her not being pushed or bullied, let alone dictated to. She had not quite used that last term, but maybe she should have... *Huuhhh.* She moaned as she finished reading the email. She decided not to answer right away, but give the man a little time, maybe, to rethink his approach, if he

could take the hint.

As much as she was scared to admit it to herself, she actually felt quite disappointed that she had not heard from Curtis, who was supposedly in Africa, as well.

A few days more went by and the situation remained static at work. She was very comfortable with her colleagues and her new boss, but started to feel less and less at ease with her crew, who were obviously firming up their position and making a point of keeping her as much on the outside as possible. The divided line that had been there from Day One was turning each day more into a trench.

The week went on and, as she sat at her computer to pay some bills and drop a note to her daughter, she saw yet another message from Chuck. She put the bills aside and opened the new email.

From: CDavies74@xxxxxx
To: Dahlfi65@xxxxxx
Subject: Hi
Date: Sunday, February 21, 10:11am

Hi, L,

Stores have been shut down here for some reason, but by tomorrow it will be opened, so I can transact. I hope you work on the issues you have at hand fast and with ease.

I will know when I will be back by tomorrow. I think we are on the same time zone now, or what is the time difference?

Waiting to read from you soon.
Chuck.

From:Dahlfi65@xxxxxx
To: Cdavies74@xxxxxx
Subject;econnections
Date Sunday, February 21, 2010 – 18:48pm

Hi, Chuck,

Glad to hear that things seem to be going well in Africa and to learn about the price of a bag of coffee beans. Anyway, I have had a full week myself and I am trouble shooting some very serious personnel issues. Not pleasant, but been there before; it just takes a lot of time, never mind personal strength and energy.

I guess you will be either back in the US or shall be travelling back shortly and that you are very much looking forward to seeing your kids.

Take care,
L.

Holly Smoke! As she had closed Chriss Muller's message she noticed caught between two spam emails, a message from Curtis Wells.

The message was short.

From: curtiswells62@xxxxxx
To: loriefinnighan@xxxxxx
Subject: econnections
Date: Sunday, February 21, 2010 – 10:30am

I have missed talking to you. Charles

Lori shut down her laptop and busied herself with her dog's walk and dinner routine, then decided to catch an early night.

6

Western Union

5:30 a.m., the damn wake-up alarm again brought her back to the world of the living. In her own mechanical, robotic way, she grabbed her first coffee and went down to her office to check her emails.

From: curtiswells@xxxxxx
To: Lorie.finnighan@xxxxxx
Subject: No subject
Date: Monday, February 22. 2010, 01:25 am

Hello, Lorie, how are you doing? Hope you had a wonderful sleep; this is the address... 10 Moore Rd., Yaba, Lagos, Nigeria. And, about when I will return your money, I will be back on March 12. I will tell you the info. you will use in sending the money through Western Union or MoneyGram.

Hope to hear from you.
Curtis.

Obviously, the man was suffering from chronic sleeping disorders, judging by the time of his email, she thought. She read through it and did not quite understand what he meant by Western Union or MoneyGram. That was the second time she had heard of Western Union. The first time,

Mathew Osborne had mentioned it to her when he had asked her in a very cavalier way to make a donation for the families following the oil platform accident.

Well, she did not know anything about Western Union and, when it came to transferring money, she was more the Swift Wire 'bank account to bank account' type of girl.

The following day, she did not think anymore of her conversation with Curtis until she got home and found a new email from him in her mailbox.

From:curtiswells62@xxxxxx
To: Lorie.finnighan@xxxxxx
Subject: HI
Date: Tuesday, February 23. 2010 4:50 pm

Hello, Laurie,

Thought I should know how my partner is faring; I hope you are not working yourself out.

Curtis.

We are being keen, she thought.

The phone rang.

"Hi, it's me; how are you?" asked Maggie.

"Not too bad; just trying to get settled in with my new company."

"And how are you finding it?" asked Maggie.

"Too early to say, really, but I can see that I am going have some hurdles along the way."

"What's that?" asked Maggie.

"People issues, Maggie; my staff. I cannot say that they are warming up to me, really," said Lorie.

"They just need a little time, that's all, Lorie. Don't let them get to you; you are better than that," said Maggie, trying to reassure her friend, as she had obviously picked up some anxieties in Lorie's voice, which was not Lorie's style at all.

"Thanks, Maggie. I will say, though, in their defence, that I am their third boss in eighteen months, so I guess they are getting a little blasé and, as far as they are concerned, before they know it, I will be gone, just like the others," said Lorie.

"I don't envy your situation, really, but if it can make you feel better, my new company is also a little strange," said Maggie.

Three months ago, Maggie had finally been asked to leave Inspect, where she had worked for Lorie for over three years prior to the merger. As Lori had been let go three months after the take over, as she was part of the senior management team, Maggie had stayed on and bought her time until they had eventually gone to her with a pay off. After taking few weeks off, Maggie had enlisted with an employment agency and very quickly found herself back in full-time employment, although it was just under a temping contract to start with.

"Hard to describe, really. People here are so serious all the time; it might be because it is a financial institution," said Maggie.

"By serious, do you mean boring?" asked Lorie.

"There is no craziness here like when we were at Inspect," said Maggie.

"I guess I can relate to what you are saying. I have not found the same buzz at PC Anywhere or Data Tech; well, if I look at my team, these guys are definitely not the happy bunch that we all were. It is sad, really. Life is hard enough without being miserable at work, Maggie."

"I agree, but you know, that's German companies for you," said Maggie.

Lori could not help bursting out laughing.

"That is fresh coming from you, German as they come,"

commented Lorie.

"Well, let say that I am just not a miserable German; that's all. I wanted to ask you, are you busy this weekend?" asked Maggie.

"Why?" asked Lorie.

"You want to come out to the country?" asked Lorie.

Maggie lived in Central Munich and prided herself as a city girl, but, from time to time, enjoyed escaping out to Dachau, which felt, for her, as if she was going to the deep countryside.

"Actually, I need a new couch," said Maggie.

"Again? So I will take that as hint that you want me to take you to Ikea, right?"

"Well, that would be nice, unless you have something else to do," said Maggie, hoping that Lorie would be free.

"That will be my pleasure; I will pack a sandwich and flask of coffee for the expedition," said Lorie in a teasing way.

Lorie never forgot the first time she had taken Maggie around Ikea. Maggie wanted some new furniture for her flat and she had never been to Ikea, so she had welcomed Lorie's offer to take her there one evening after work.

As Maggie was diligently going around the store, examining, very carefully, each piece of furniture that she was looking to acquire, constantly retracing her steps as she wanted to double check again on that cream sofa, and 'maybe that would look nice with the coffee table that I saw one floor down' as Maggie would comment while pursuing her shopping quest.

Lorie had recognised very quickly after entering the store and observing the shopping ritual of her friend that they would be there for the long haul, and adopted the approach of finding the best chair she could find in every section they were going through, and just parked herself and kept busy with her blackberry and work emails.

As Maggie had made her selection, they went through the check-out counter and headed to the service counter to organise for the furniture to be delivered to Maggie's apartment. As the man informed Maggie that the next available date would be the following Tuesday, Maggie had turned around to Lorie and asked if she could take the day off.

Lorie smiled and agreed after commenting on the fact it was somewhat convenient for one to have their boss at hand whilst shopping for bulky items.

"No problem, Maggie, Ikea it is on Saturday. I will be doing my usual morning round, so I can pick you up at the subway station early afternoon. Does that work for you?" asked Lorie.

"Sure. I will send you an SMS when I am on the train to let you know what time I will be there," said Maggie.

"Okay, then, I will see you on Saturday. Have a good rest of the week, Maggie, and thanks for the call," said Lorie.

Lorie put down the phone and headed to the kitchen to feed her two hungry companions, after which she logged onto her laptop and sent a quick message to Curtis.

To: curtiswells62@xxxxxx
From: Lorie.finnighan@xxxxxx
Subject: Hi
Date: Tuesday, February 23, 2010 08:31pm

Hello, partner,
I forgot to say in my previous email. Here is my home number if you want to call: +49 xx xx xxx xxx

    It might be very expensive from Lagos; not sure, but up to you. I think I have found a solution for you.

Take care,
Lorie.

Lorie carried on working whilst monitoring to see if Curtis was going to come online, as she wanted to talk to him about transferring the cash so that he could get his pumps to California. She was interested and curious about his business, as it was completely different to her professional corporate world.

As she was getting tired and Curtis still had not showed, she decided to drop him another email.

From: Loriefinnighan@xxxxxx
To: curtiswells@xxxxxx
Subject: Hi
Date: Tuesday, February 23 2010 10:52pm

Hi, Curtis,

I was hoping to connect with you tonight, but you might have been busy. Anyway, if you still need a hand with bringing your pumps back. My idea is that I can go to the airport on my way back from work and see if I can send you the cash from there.

I cannot get on messenger in the office, so send me an email. Also, see herewith my mobile number, +49 xxx xx xx xxx, just in case.

Cu partner!

After writing the email, Lorie closed her laptop and went to bed.

5:30 a.m., rise and shine! Lorie had set herself to be in the office as early as possible that day, as she had a lot to get on with. It had been snowing all the through the night, which was not what she needed on that day. She jumped out of bed and, whilst her morning coffee was slowly brewing, she proceeded to get dressed in order not to waste time.

By the time she got back down to the kitchen, her coffee was ready in the pot. She poured herself a cup and decided to go check her emails to see if Curtis had replied to her.

She was relieved that there was no comeback from Chuck Davies, and somewhat happy to find one from Curtis Wells, which had come in during the night.

To: loriefinnighan@xxxxxx
From: curtiswells62@xxxxxx
Subject: Hi
Date: Tuesday, February 23. 11:53pm

Hello, Laurie,

How are you doing; missed you, too. I have been too busy; I am sorry. You said you will go to the airport to send the money; really, when I read that I was just laughing, because that is one of the weirdest things to even think of. I can really place a bet on the fact that the money will never get to me.

Lorie, the best thing is through a money transfer agent; Western Union is the best for me here, 'cos they are closer around here.

I will be looking forward to hearing from you and I know you are quite busy, but I really must tell you that is the only way I can get the money and be sure it will get to me, so please think about it, 'cos I really do not want a situation where someone will lose money here. I am sure you can find a way to try to send it, even with your busy schedule.

Thanks and hope to talk to you soon.

Best regards,
Curtis.

Hmm, she thought. *Who does he think he is, as well, trying to tell me what to do?* She would get back to him once in the office. She shut down her laptop, went back up to the hallway, put her snow boots on, and on cue, she heard the huffing and puffing and the sound of a wagging tale against the banister behind her. Baberuth had finally dragged himself out of bed and was giving her signs that he was ready, whilst Lady got herself busy trying to chew his ankles. Lorie was amazed at how much abuse the big beast was taking from the little pooch without any retaliation whatsoever.

She enjoyed the snowy weather and the peacefulness it gave to the landscape, especially in the early hours of the day when she was probably the only insane person to be walking her dogs under heavy snow at that time of the morning…

Due to the heavy falls during the night, getting to the office took her longer than she had accounted for, but, before getting busy with her morning tasks, she dropped a quick note back to Curtis to set him straight, too.

To:curtiswells62@xxxxxx
From:loriefinnighan@xxxxxx
Subject:Hi
Date:Wednesday, February 24, 08 30:53am

Hi, Curtis,

There was nothing funny about my suggestion. They have Reisen Bank there, which is open quite late. I am just trying to help out, so don't make fun of my creativity. I have explained to you that there is no way I can get to the city.

Sorry, and, for my busy schedule, I am leaving my house at 7 a.m. and not getting back home before 8 p.m., so my apologies if you don't find me flexible enough.

Take care.

Having survived another day with the Hell team, she decided to cut it short due to the bad weather and get back home a little bit earlier. Whilst getting on with the compulsory greeting of Baberuth and Lady, she quickly went through her post and put it down as fast as she had picked it up as, from the colours of the envelopes, there was, for sure, no good news inside. So, she pushed the letters on the 'do it at the weekend' pile.

After attending to the dinners, she went down to her office and set up her work laptop, as she needed to prepare a PowerPoint presentation, but, before getting down to business, she quickly checked her private email and decided to answer Chuck Davies, whom had emailed her a couple of days earlier.

From: Dahlfi65@xxxxxx
To: Cdavies74@xxxxxx
Subject: Hi
Date: Wednesday, February 24, 19:50

Hi, Chuck,

Hope that the stores did re-open so that you could transact, as you had put it. Work is pretty consuming right now, but hopefully things will eventually bed down, which will give me a bit more free space.

Where about are you in Africa? Africa is more or less in the same time zone, depending on when you are, of course. You are probably looking forward to going home and telling all the coffee beans to your boys.

If you are ready to head back, then I wish you a pleasant and safe trip home.

Kr
L

As she was sweating away at her presentation, an email came in. She opened her mailbox.

Well, well, she thought. *He did not waste any time, did he now!* She opened the email and started to read.

From: cdavies74@xxxxxx
To: Lorie.finnighan@xxxxxx
Re: Hi
Date: Wednesday, February 24, 2010 08:36 pm

Hello, Lorie

Am really happy to read from you right now. I was actually in great jeopardy about a present issue I am facing now; I actually got what I am here to purchase, and I tried to access my account from here, but I couldn't. I even tried to use my credit card and I also couldn't; am really confused right now. I told my mom's sister in the state about this issue, and she tried today to go to my bank and look for a way she could access my account, and she wasn't allowed to do that and, on this same issue, my credit card was blocked for security purposes, so you see what is going on now. I am actually in Nigeria, and yeah, I checked online now and I see you're on the same time zone; I don't think I am ready to go back right now, because I don't even have enough finances with me anymore to mobilise myself here, and all the bags have been loaded and sealed; I just have to pay now. Well, my mom's sister said she will see tomorrow if she can get some amount sent to me from a private account she got, but she also said she can't promise if it will be up to the actual amount I need. The total amount I need now to pay for the cocoa beans is $45,000, including shipping and all. I know you're really not the best person to include on the list of people who can help me, because I will start making some calls, too, but I wouldn't mind if you can help me in any way you can; I will really appreciate that, but know fully well that no matter the amount you will be lending me, I will definitely pay you back, okay. I *have a number you can reach me on here: +234xxxxxx. Please, I will try to give you a call now, but please, if you can call me, too, because I don't have much finance anymore at hand; thanks for your understanding, my friend.*

Chuck

"What the hell!" she exclaimed.

She had a hard time grasping the whole content of the email, so she read it, read it again, and one more time just to be sure that she had got the correct understanding of the long message. Yep, she had.

This guy has got some nerve!

Then, without any second thoughts, she pressed the 'reply' button and threw back a one liner at him:

From Dahlfi65@xxxxxx
To: Cdavies74@xxxxxx
Subject: Hi
Date: Wednesday February 24, 08:54pm

Oh, and I let me guess, I will need to go the Western Union bank to transfer the cash, right?

L.

Still under the shock of Chuck's somewhat direct email, she carried on with her work, and not much time elapsed before he responded back to her:

To: Cdavies74@xxxxxx
From: Dahlfi65@xxxxxx
Subject: Hi
Date: Wednesday February 24.2010 09:21pm

Are you kidding with me, or are you being serious that you will help me? C.

Hey! is this guy for real or what? Time to put that one to bed before someone gets hurt, she told to herself, and wrote back.

From: Dahlfi65@xxxxxx
To: Cdavies74@xxxxxx
Subject: Hi
Date:Wednesday February 24 ,10:05pm

I am sorry, Chuck, but no can do. I was just being sarcastic, as you are the third guy this week who happens to be in Africa and asked me to send him cash, but, of course, I need to go the Western Union.

Sorry, it might be harsh, but frankly, I just could not believe it when I saw your email...

Lorie

"There! Get back on your horse, Partner!" she said as she was pressing the send button.

The man was obviously not taking no for an answer, as he had pushed, yet again, another note back to her.

From: Cdavies74@xxxxxx
To: Dahlfi65@xxxxxx
Subject: Hi
Date: Wednesday February 24, 11:01pm

What do you mean someone in Africa asked you for money? Because I need financial help from you, you compare me to your friends in Africa? Be straight and tell me you can't help me rather than comparing me to people.

Hello! What is this guy on, she wondered.

"Okay, then, obviously I was not clear enough," Lorie commented to herself. "And what does 'HW' stand for, anyway? Howdy? Well, howdy to you, too, cowboy!"

I will take care of his case in the morning, she told herself, bringing down her computer for a well-earned rest, too.

* * *

5:30 a.m. – The unforgivable ring of the alarm cut through the silence of her bedroom like razor blades.

As she diligently went through her morning ritual of drinking first coffee whilst checking her emails, the somewhat interesting exchange that she had had the night before with Chuck Davies came back to her, and she got down to business and wrote back to him.

From:Dahlfi65@xxxxxx
To:Cdavies74@xxxxxx
Subject:Hi
Date: Wednesday February 24th 05:52 am

Chuck,

I was being straight by saying no can do… Just funny that it happened three times this week; that's all… Sorry.

Lorie

Feeling quite proud of herself, she kitted up and went for a morning walk with Baberuth and Lady.

Later on, as she was driving to work, she could not help but process again the communications that she had had with Chuck and Curtis, both being in Africa, both seeming to have got themselves in a muddle, somewhat. For all that she knew, they could be one and the same person, really. She had made the decision that she would assist Curtis as, for one reason or another, she felt more comfortable with him than with Chuck, whose somewhat controlling, short-fused personality had come out quite early in their prior communications. She told herself that she would call Sophie that evening and relate her interesting experience to her.

As s her team had gone out for an early lunch, she decided to check her emails to see if she had received any news from Curtis, from whom she had not heard since she had agreed to help him.

"I don't believe it!" she exclaimed as she found a fresh email from Chuck Davies, whom obviously could not possibly know how to read.

From:Cdavies74@xxxxxx
To: Dahlfi65@xxxxxx
Subject: Hi
Date: Thursday February 25.2010 09:51am

There's no way you can assist, right?
Chuck.

This time, he was really pushing it, she thought, and, since the man did not seem to understand 'no', she decided to rough him up a little bit more.

To: Dahlfi65@xxxxxx
From: Cdavies74@xxxxxx
Subject: Hi
Date: Thursday February 25.2010 12:15pm

Oh, Chuck, unfortunately someone has beaten you to that goal post... Sorry, I am not the European Central Reserve Bank.

Lorie.

The tones of the emails that she had received from both Chuck and Curtis really rubbed her the wrong way. That is what you get for trying to help out, she thought.

After yet another exciting day at the office trying to bring down the Berlin Wall, which seemed to have erupted over the past couple of weeks with her team, and spending hours in her boss' office debating how they should move on with the situation, Lorie decided that she would call it a day and finish what she needed to finish at home. The snow had not stopped the whole day, and she braced herself for the drive back home, which was bound to take a lot longer.

As she finally turned the corner of her street, she screamed, "Oh, no! Not tonight!"

The snow plough had obviously come around and had pushed the pile of snow across her driveway, thus somewhat blocking the access to her garage, which was right at the corner of the street. She had many time before abused the driver verbally for just discarding the load he had dragged from the street in front of her driveway, completely blocking the access to her garage in the process.

As she was slowly driving up towards her garage, she was assessing whether or not she could force the car in without having to spend the next thirty minutes shuffling away to clear the passage. She got closer and, in a fit of temper, gave full power to get the vehicle over the mount of snow. Luckily for her, the snow barrier was not as high as she had anticipated. It was still quite fresh and soft, which allowed her to get the car in, leaving behind two very clean-cut tyre trails.

After going through the greeting dance with her two dogs and feeding them their dinner, she went down to her office and booted up her home laptop.

She found an email from Curtis, which had come during the afternoon.

To: loriefinnighan@xxxxxx
From: curtiswells@xxxxxx
Subject: Hi
Date: Thursday February 25.,2010 16:43pm

Hello, Lorie,

Still laughing about the email you sent to me, lol; I just didn't know what to say, 'cos it was quite funny; well, honey, if the banks there have Western Union, then it is cool, because the best way for me to receive the money is through Western Union and I really do not want to be in a situation where money will be lost...
       This is the information you will use in sending the money:

Name: Curtis Wells
City: Yaba
State: Lagos
Country: Nigeria
Zip code: 23401
Test question: son's name?
Test answer: Joshua

Lorie, after sending, you will have to give me the sender's information (name and address) and also the MTCN that will be on the money transfer receipt, and also, if you did use another thing for the 'test question and answer', you will have to email that to me, 'cos I will need that with my ID to receive the money here.
       Hope to hear from you soon, dear, and it was good that you were creative :)

Best regards,
Curtis.

Lorie diligently read the email and liked the fact that Curtis was using his son's name as the secret question. In one of his first emails to Lorie, Curtis had mentioned the fact that he was divorced and that he had full custody of his son. Lorie had sensibly questioned him on that as, although not uncommon, it is a fact that, in most divorce cases, the mother tends to get full custody of the child or children over the father. Curtis had explained to Lorie that his wife had left him for another man and that she had never really intended to have children in the first place. Since that time, Curtis had raised his son single-handedly. She understood how difficult it was being a single parent, as she had been one herself since the death of husband, but she believed that it was a lot harder for a man than a woman to handle such a situation.

7

Lost in the Post

There is lot to be said about being two when it comes to raising a child. Through the online chats and the emails, Lorie had sensed that Curtis was longing for a family, not just for himself, but more so for his little boy. Lorie did miss having her husband around and it had taken her a very long time to realise that he would never come home again. There was nothing strange for her to be home without him, as he tended to travel regularly for his job, the same as she did. So, once she had got past the initial shock of that tragic Sunday afternoon, she kept on with her routines, with only one objective in mind: providing her daughter with security. Lorie and her husband had moved around a lot over the years and never stayed more than four years in the same place, as they were constantly trying to keep up with work and life demands. All those tough years as a single parent, wanting to keep her daughter stable, resurfaced overnight with Curtis discussing his son with her.

Processing through her head what it would mean, should they come together, she could not help seeing the challenges of them bringing their lives together due to her job. But then, again, being a stay-at-home mummy sounded real sweet to her. When she had registered on the online dating website to find a potential companion, she had not considered that the companion in question may come with little people in tow. This was a total new aspect for her to consider, but that would by no means be a deal breaker. After all, Curtis did imply that she would not have to work anymore, as he wanted to look after his woman, as he had put it to her. Nevertheless, a little boy added to the mix was something she had to take very seriously and, from what she had gathered so far, Curtis seemed to be a bit of child himself, with lots of dreams and fantasies, which she associated with high maintenance. As far as she was concerned, she was done with husband sitting, as John, her late husband, had proven very hard work at times, to the point where the marriage nearly did not survive. To the very end, John had kept her busy and running around as he nearly missed his own funeral.

After John had passed away, Lorie was faced with the decision of where John should be laid to rest and, after consorting with her mother, they decided that although John was British, he would be put to rest with Lorie's dad in France, as they were extremely close. At the time, John's parents were away in Australia and, completely overwhelmed by the situation. She had no choice but to make a quick decision, which was, to her relief, appreciated by his parents.

The morning before the funeral, Lorie received a called from the funeral home informing her that the urn had not arrived. In a panic, she jumped in her car and drove to the funeral home to see what was going on.

She sat with the man in charge, checked all the transport papers and saw something that made her turn as white as a sheet. In disbelief, she drove back home to call the funeral home in Germany, which had organised the transport of the ashes..

"Hello, could I speak to Gisela Witman, please?"

"Speaking, how can I help you?"

"This is Lorie Finnighan, here. You organised for the ashes of my husband, John, to be sent to France."

"Yes, that is right. What can I do?"

"Well, the urn has not arrived yet and the funeral home in France is getting nervous, as they were expecting it yesterday afternoon."

"I am deeply sorry; let me check the papers."

"Actually, I have the papers in front of me and I cannot see any kind of tracking reference. May I ask how you sent it?"

"Well, we sent the urn by registered post, I can track it to the border, but, after that, we have no way to locate where it is at the moment."

"You *did what*?" Lorie screamed at the woman. "Registered post? What is wrong with you people? I would have expected for the urn to be couriered. These are my husband's ashes we are talking about, not some kind of gift parcel!"

"I am really sorry; I don't know what I can do."

"I will contact the postal offices here, but do rest assured that this conversation is far from being over," said Lorie as she put the phone down.

As she turned around, she saw ten pairs of eyes staring at her. Her family had obviously picked up on the fact that there was an issue, but, as they did not understand the conversation that had taken place in English, they were standing around her with questioning faces.

Not knowing what to say, Lorie faced them and said, "John is lost in the post; I need to go to the main post office to see if they have him."

Without waiting for their reaction, she grabbed her car keys and, accompanied by her closest cousin for moral support, she drove to the triage centre in town.

"Good afternoon; how can I help you?" asked the postal agent behind the counter.

"Well, I am not sure how to put this, but you would not have received my husband through the post last night, by any chance? He is about this high and that wide," said Lorie, using her hands to describe the parcel.

The man looked at her quizzically, not really sure what to make of this strange request. Reading his face, Lorie pulled the transports papers and explained the situation to him.

"I am sorry, Madam Finnighan, we have not received such a parcel, but please let me take your number and let me give you a number in return, which you can call from 5 a.m. tomorrow, if we have not been successful in locating the ashes by then."

Realising that there was nothing left she could do other than wait, the two women went back to the house to talk to the family and explain the situation. Drama, drama, drama was all over the house, as her mother and John's were completely falling apart. Not able to cope with the mayhem, Lorie picked up the phone and, locking herself in her bedroom, dialled Micky's number.

Micky had been Lorie's boss for many years, and they were still actively working together, as well as being close friends.

"Hi, Micky, it is Lorie."

"Oh, hi girl, how are you keeping?" he asked

"Not sure, really; you will never guess what is going on."

"What's that?"

"John has been lost in the post. We do not know where the urn is, as that stupid funeral home in Germany sent the ashes through normal post."

"You are kidding me?"

"I wish I was."

"Well, we are actually about to leave to catch the ferry to come to you and, as it so happens, we had a BBQ last night, so should I bring some ashes for contingency?" asked Micky.

That was so typical of Micky, thought Lorie, but she just could not help but burst out laughing at the suggestion. Her nerves were getting the better of her; that was clear.

The next morning, dead on 5 a.m., Lorie dialled the number to the triage centre and went through her speech about the lost urn.

The man asked her very nicely to stay on the line, after which he proceeded, obviously, by turning around to his colleagues, and asked them in a loud voice if they could look for a parcel from Germany to the name of Finnighan. It did not take long before Lorie heard a voice coming from behind, shouting, "*I have it!*"

Lorie had this vision of the ashes of her deceased husband being berried between Amazon and Victoria's Secret parcels. Then again, knowing John the way she did, he would have probably enjoyed that.

John had kept her running to the bitter end. Curtis's childlike ways had raised red flags, however, they were still in the process of finding out about each other and she was not going to jump to a foregone conclusion.

8

Erdinger Str. 45b, Berglern

Lorie spent the night tossing and turning, as she just could not seem to be able to find sleep. Curtis' emails kept rewriting themselves through her mind as if the cursor of her brain had been kept pressed down constantly, bringing her thoughts back to the beginning of the message. The communication dynamic that she and Curtis had grown into over the previous weeks made her more and more comfortable with him, but that night, it hit her like lightning. She had never met him.

On one hand, she liked the idea of her newfound business partnership, but, on the other hand, she felt that it might be a good idea to seek out a little bit more information before parting with her hard-earned money. Eventually, she managed to doze off, but her restlessness and curiosity somewhat kicked her out of bed before the dreaded alarm had a chance to come on.

"Take that, sunshine!" Lorie said to the alarm as she switched off the evil device before it kicked in.

Whilst the coffee percolator was getting busy making her hot, fresh morning brew, she sat at her computer and wrote a note to Curtis.

From: loriefinnighan@xxxxxx
To: curtiswell@xxxxxx
Subject: Western Union
Date: Friday, February 26, 2010 5:12am

Hi, Curtis,

I am prepared to wire the cash to you today. But first, please give me your home address in Germany and telephone number.
Also, let me know when you will be back in Germany and how you intend to get the cash back to me.
I know I am being a pain in the backside over this, but, for now, as far as I am concerned, you are just this guy I got to know over an Internet dating website.
Up to you.

L

She thought that it might be good to make a point to Curtis that she had very little to go on when it came to who he was and she therefore took the opportunity to remind him how they got connected.

On that email, she left for work after her usual walk around the field with the two pooches. Driving along, she made a mental note that she should call her daughter, Jane.

As she was keeping herself occupied at her desk, she was observing the chaos going around her. Her loyal team was busy clearing desks and putting files in boxes. She had heard that the department was being moved from the fifth floor down to the first floor, but no one had approached her to discuss it. Despite her poor German, she had caught peaces of information, in passing conversations between her team members on the topic, but had made a point not to approach them on the topic to see if, eventually, they would come to her to discuss it. The move had been decided prior her joining the company and had been only mentioned here and there over the weeks running up to that day. As she had not received any direct communication from anyone about it, she had not given it any more thoughts until that very moment.

She carried on working away, ignoring the situation purposely until, eventually, the facility manager stood at her desk telling her that she needed to pack up her stuff as they had to move her desk to the first floor. She looked up at him and, in a very defying way, instructed him to come back later.

He told her that it was not possible as he had a tight schedule and that the move had been planned for that morning, so he needed her to clear her desk.

Lorie could no longer contain her anger and told him that no one had consorted with her about this and, therefore, he should come back later. The facility manager pushed back on her, informing her that Melanie had discussed and agreed on the date and time with him.

For Lorie, that was the last drop, and she totally lost her temper and asked the facility guy since when they were making agreements and taking instructions from a staff member without the department manager's approval.

After few more brutal verbal exchanges, Lorie stood and decided to take a walk down to the new office to see what she was being faced with. It took her less than five seconds to assess that the floor plan would not exactly work for her, and she decided to go up to her boss' office to relay to him what had just happened.

Karl was fuming and ran downstairs to evaluate the situation. The way the A-Team had strategically placed their desks was implying that the only place for Lorie's desk would be literally in the doorway, with her back to the room entrance.

Karl took no prisoners and gave the three rebels a verbal

lashing that Lorie would not have imagined him capable of.

She felt absolutely disgusted by the behaviour and defiance of the very people whose jobs she was trying to protect. The line had been drawn there and then in the sand; the road ahead would be very bumpy, as far as Lorie was concerned, but she was not prepared to back down as she really loved her job and needed stability professionally, at least, for three to four years. So the knives had been pulled out and the fight was on.

Having wasted literally the whole day performing crisis management, all Lorie wanted to do was to head straight for bed after she got home; however, she was behind and needed to catch up on her work emails.

Whilst her work laptop was going through the loading screens, she opened her Yahoo mailbox on her home laptop and found an email from Curtis. With Nigeria being one hour behind Germany, she could not help but notice the early hour of Curtis' email, which surprised her, as he tended to be more of a midnight owl than an early bird. He must have picked up on her email shortly after she had sent it to him that very morning.

From:curtiswells@xxxxxx
To: Lorie.finnighan@xxxxxx
Subject:Western Union
Date:Friday, February 27. 2010 06:47 am

Hello, L

I am sorry that I didn't get back to you earlier…
Here is my address: Erdinger Str. 45b, 85459 Berglern, and my number, 08762426200, is not going through at the moment, 'cos it is currently disconnected because of the trip. I will be back by the second week of March, and then I will repay; we can arrange a meeting so I will give you the money or I can wire it to you; any way you want. Hope to hear from

you soon, and the name, Webby, really got me laughing hard.

Thanks,
Curtis.

During the previous night's short online conversation, Lorie had referred to him as Webby on the basis that she had met him on the Web. She liked the idea that he obviously welcomed her sense of humour.

His email was re-assuring to her, but, to get final comfort, she Googled the address.

Well, what do you know, she thought. As she examined the Google map, it transpired that Berglern was on her side of town and just passed the airport. It could not be better, as far as she was concerned, and she proceeded by responding to him.

From: Lorie.finnighan@xxxxxx
To: curtiswells@xxxxxx
Subject: Western Union
Date: Friday, February 26. 2010 09:58pm

Believe it or not, but I just picked up your email. I was in the office until 9:30 tonight, as I have had a day in Hell and I am not looking forward to Monday, as it is promising to be quite violent.

I will go to the airport tomorrow and do the wire for you (DON'T CROSS ME! I have had a shitty week), as I need to pick up my Goldy Buddy from the TierHotel in Halbergmoos. Why is he in the Tier Hotel? Because he was in LOVE. My little dog, Lady, who was actually schedule to be spayed today, decided that it was LOVE SEASON last Monday. Tuesday and Wednesday night, no one slept, as Baberuth Sex Machine had ideas of his own and sassy Lady was being the tease of the century, so, by Thursday morning, I had arranged for my neighbour to take Buddy to his favourite pension for a few days so that we could all get some sleep.

I am hoping that everything will be back to normal tomorrow.

Lorie

After coming home, Lorie made a point of calling Maggie to confirm their shopping appointment for the following day. The two women spoke for a while, both sharing with each other their work trials and tribulations, but at no point did Lorie mention to Maggie her side activities with Curtis.

Later on that evening, she received a call from Sophie, from whom she had not heard for while. Lorie appreciated the long-distance friendship she shared with Sophie. Despite the geographical distance, the two women were very close, as each one felt she could relate to other one's life situation. Sophie, just like Lorie, had had her life entirely controlled by her job, and the two women enjoyed dwelling and debating during their long phone conversations on the challenges of being a mid-forty-something single working girl. Although Sophie had never been married, she had had a relationship that had lasted literally as long as Lorie's marriage. The relationship had ended several years ago, and, since then, Sophie, like Lorie, had just been giving her life away to whatever firm she happened to be working for.

As Lorie felt more comfortable discussing her love life, or lack thereof, with Sophie, she introduced Curtis to her, but would not mention at this stage that she had offered financial support to the man in question.

As they were bouncing back their thoughts on work life or just life on the phone, Lorie saw her messenger coming to life.

CURTIS WELLS (2/26/2010 2:16:20 AM): *Hello, you there?*
CURTIS WELLS (2/26/2010 11:19:25 PM): *Hello.*

CURTIS WELLS (2/26/2010 11:21:08 PM): *hey dearie*
CURTIS WELLS (2/26/2010 11:21:19 PM): *laughing about your dog lol*
CURTIS WELLS (2/26/2010 11:21:22 PM): *just read your email*
CURTIS WELLS (2/26/2010 11:43:38 PM): *hey you there*

"How about that?" Lorie asked Sophie on the phone. "Talking about the Devil; he has just appeared on messenger."

"Really! I better let you go, but do keep me posted. I am curious to see how this is going to develop," said Sophie.

"I will, Sophie. Have a nice weekend," ended Lorie.

Lorie read through the cascade of messages that Curtis had sent, obviously eager to make contact, and she had an idea of the reason why the man got so active suddenly on messenger. She toyed for a few minutes to acknowledge him or maybe not. As she did not want to him think she was shutting him down, she left her computer online and went up to get ready for bed without answering him. She would go back down and switch it off later.

* * *

The early morning winter sun coming through the bay window of Lorie's bedroom brought her back slowly to the world of the livings whilst, obviously, Lady was already all fired up and ready for action. Lorie tried to give Lady a good morning cuddle, but the little bomb on legs had other ideas in mind.

"All right, then, Lady, I have got the message," said Lorie to Lady as she was getting up and putting on her dressing gown. "Why don't you go out in the garden for a little bit, Lady, and guess what?" said Lorie to the little beast, who was attentively listening to her, her ears perked up. "Today, Mummy is going to go and pick up Baberuth. That will be good to have him back home, don't you think?"

Lady was doing a funny dance around Lorie as if she was trying to show her approval.

Two weeks prior, Lorie had had to take Baberuth to the TierHotel by the airport as co-habitation was not going to be bearable for a short while, as Lady had come on heat prematurely. Lorie was fuming as she had actually scheduled Lady to be spayed that very week, but, as everything in her current life, things were obviously not going to go according to plan; why should they?

Lorie still had vivid memories of suffering Baberuth being love, as she called it, in the first few days of January a few years ago, whilst her mother had come over the Christmas holidays. It was total chaos in the house, as Baberuth was going completely out of his skin and driving the rest of the house out of theirs in the process. It was clear that the night was bound to be tough between Baberuth panting around the house all night long and mother adding to the situation by spitting out her jelly fish comments one after the other; Lorie needed to find a solution to bring the situation at end under control.

As her mother had finally gone up to bed, and Baberuth had obviously no intention of calming down, as he was trying to mount anything he could jump on, her first idea was to take him for a drive in the car. It was close to midnight and the roads were not that brilliant, but she would keep to the main arteries. As she was driving away from the neighbourhood, Baberuth had relaxed more and eventually ended upl asleep on the back seat of the car. She drove up to the next gas station, went in to get a coffee, and sat back in her car, her warm cup in hand. She looked at her dog, completely spread out on the back seat, and obviously enjoying a good old snooze, judging by the snoring going on.

Typical, she thought. *Okay, what now,* she asked herself. First thing first; she needed to get back home, as it was nearly 2 a.m., and she had to go back to work the following day.

As Baberuth did not stir one bit as she slowly pulled into the garage, she decided to stay with him in the car to ensure he would not end up going crazy again, destroying the inside of her BMW in the process. Luckily, she had put her ski suit on and she had a blanket on the back seat, which she reached for and managed to tear away from the big sleeping dog. No, Lorie would not forget the night she had slept in her car with her dog because of love.

This time around, with Lady right under the same roof, She did not think twice and, at the first opportunity, took Baberuth to his pension, but she could not wait to get him back home and she had it in mind already to go and pick him up that very day.

After religiously grabbing her first coffee, she went down to her computer and checked her email.

From: curtiswells62@xxxxxx
To: loriefinnighan@xxxxxx
Subject: Western Union
Date: Friday February 26. 2010 15:06pm

Hello, L,

How are you doing; thanks so much for the email... I knew you would probably have a very hectic day. I thought you were online, saw ya online and thought we will be able to talk; anyway, it was an Islamic holiday here. So I was in and looked forward to talking to you.

Really laughing about your dogs; I would love to meet them.

Hope to hear from you soon...

Kindest regards,
Curtis

Although she enjoyed receiving the email, she could not help but think that the reason for so much attention was due to the fact that she had offered to help him out financially.

She finished her coffee, shut down her laptop and jumped in the shower, as she was going to be late again for her Bikini Unfit Class, as she called it. After her workout and her shopping, she went to pick up Maggie from the subway station, and they set off for Ikea as they had planned.

To Lorie's relief, the second Ikea expedition did not take as long as the first one and, after sharing a pot of tea and cake, Lorie dropped Maggie back at the nearest subway station before carrying on to the airport to pick up Baberuth.

What the heck, she thought; since she was on airport ground, she might as well go to the Western Union counter and send the cash to Curtis. After all, she had committed to help him, so either she went through with it or she needed to tell him that the offer was off the table. The constant 'should I or shouldn't I' was driving her nuts, so it was time to close this semi-trauma she was continuously inflicting on herself and move on, she decided.

As she returned back to her car, she felt a chill down her back, turning over and over again in her head what the Western Union agent had said to her.

She spent the whole night hovering around the house, not knowing anymore what to do. She would sleep on it and re-assess in the morning.

* * *

Something or, rather, someone, was scratching her head. As she turned over in her bed, she found herself nose to nose with Lady, who was standing right above her face delicately scratching her head with her little paw, as if to say, 'you're awake? C'mon already, get up, get up'. Lorie had no choice but to comply with the demands of the little pooch as, obviously, Lady had some urgent business to attend to in the garden. Baberuth, on the other hand, was spread at the bottom of the bed and showed no sign whatsoever of wanting to jump to action.

Lorie opened the patio doors to let Lady out and made her way to the kitchen to get her first coffee of the day. After Lady had come back in, they went down to the office and armed with a good night of sleep, she wrote an email to Curtis.

From: loriefinnighan@xxxxxx
To: curtiswells@xxxxxx
Subject: Western Union
Date: Sunday February 28, 2010 08:33am

Hi, C,

Went to the Reisen Bank yesterday, got the form, and then the lady asked if the money would be taken out in USD or local currency. I did not know and, since I did not have a contact number for you in Nigeria, I put the form in my handbag.

But, she also asked me why I was transferring so much money and if I knew the person. She said that they are asking everyone this question as, apparently, there is a big scam going on at the moment where some dishonest individuals connect with people on the Internet, then give them made-up stories to get them to send cash to them using Western Union. You would not know anything about that, would you? You need to look at this from my point of view here... After all, you are the third Internet guy in a row who ends up in Nigeria and asked me to send them cash...

Curtis, I have had a really shitty week; losing two thousand euro to a crook would just top it all, so convince me real good why I should help you here. I need to go back to the airport at the end of this afternoon to take Buddy back to his pension, as the doggies are still going mental, so let me know.

I will check in thirty minutes if you are online or not; otherwise, let me know when you will be.

CU
L

Lorie was not happy about having to write such an email, but, on the other hand, she could not get past what the lady at the WU counter had told her, so she felt she needed to put it out there to the man and see how he would react. If he was to stop all contact the way Mathew Osborne had done, that would represent in her mind an admission of ill intentions by default.

Whilst she kept herself busy with her housework, her mother rang. As usual, they chit chatted about the weather, Jane, and the family. Lorie would not breeze a word to her mother about her current dilemma as, for sure, it would worry the old lady endless, let alone the fact that, for sure, her mother would not understand what could possibly drive Lorie to agree to do such a thing for someone she had never met.

The fact that she had never met Curtis, yet that she felt so comfortable with him, was a strange concept to her, and she enjoyed their email exchange and the random messenger conversations she had had with him so far.

After showering, she put Baberuth in the back of her car, direction Tierhotel; there was still too much love in the house, so it was clear that the lovebirds needed to be parted for a little while longer.

Once back home, she grabbed a quick ball of cornflakes and got busy catching up on her housework, which had been heavily compromised by Lady and Baberuth's activities. She put a load in her washing machine and, as she was busy clearing her desk, she saw her messenger flashing. Curtis was online and pinging her for a chat.

CURTIS WELLS (2/28/2010 3:41:54 PM): *Hello L*

LORIE.FINNIGHAN (2/28/2010 3:42:12 PM): *Hi Hang on. I need to go and get my glasses*

LORIE.FINNIGAN (2/28/2010 3:43:45 PM): *How are you?*

CURTIS WELLS (2/28/2010 3:44:14 PM): *I am good*

CURTIS WELLS (2/28/2010 3:44:21 PM): *do you use glasses on computer*

LORIE.FINNIGHAN (2/28/2010 3:44:45 PM): *Yep, I do, is this an issue?*

CURTIS WELLS (2/28/2010 3:45:18 PM): *nope it is not, I actually did darken the brightness of my computer*

CURTIS WELLS (2/28/2010 3:45:24 PM): *so I will not have problems with my eyes*

LORIE.FINNIGHAN (2/28/2010 3:46:06 PM): *I saw your email thanks*

CURTIS WELLS (2/28/2010 3:46:43 PM): *you're welcome*

CURTIS WELLS (2/28/2010 3:48:07 PM): *how is your Sunday*

LORIE.FINNIGHAN (2/28/2010 3:49:19 PM): *Well I have had better ones for sure...I had to take Baberuth back at lunch time as it was total chaos still, let alone that the last week at work is still haunting me and I really don't know what I am going find tomorrow*

LORIE.FINNIGHAN (2/28/2010 3:50:10 PM): *Look, I will help you out with the 2K in good faith and goodwill and to convince me that there are still people worthy of my trust around...*

CURTIS WELLS (2/28/2010 3:50:24 PM): *thanks Lorie*

LORIE.FINNIGHAN (2/28/2010 3:51:12 PM): *I am kind of hoping that this little friendship deal will lead to a very nice friendship as per we can help each out on our spare time and have fun doing it*

CURTIS WELLS (2/28/2010 3:51:47 PM): *yes you are right, I am really getting more into you*

LORIE.FINNIGHAN (2/28/2010 3:52:27 PM): *get out of town, wise guy,*

LORIE.FINNIGHAN (2/28/2010 3:52:38 PM): *we have not even met yet*

LORIE.FINNIGHAN (2/28/2010 3:53:00 PM): *I don't believe that few messages can connect people*

CURTIS WELLS (2/28/2010 3:53:43 PM): *well that is why I am looking forward to meeting you*

LORIE.FINNIGHAN (2/28/2010 3:55:47 PM): *I have no expectations as far as a romantic future with you, but having a nice friend would be really nice*

CURTIS WELLS (2/28/2010 3:56:05 PM): *sure it will be nice*

LORIE.FINNIGHAN (2/28/2010 3:56:54 PM): *you could come around and cut my lawn on Saturdays and I could help you out with your house cleaning and we could have BBQs in my back garden and enjoy a nice evening and bullshit conversation*

CURTIS WELLS (2/28/2010 4:01:14 PM): *yes that is cool*

CURTIS WELLS (2/28/2010 4:01:22 PM): *I am sure you can be a good friend to Joshua too*

LORIE.FINNIGHAN (2/28/2010 4:01:38 PM): *so, when are you getting back to Munich exactly?*

LORIE.FINNIGHAN (2/28/2010 4:06:25 PM): *How old is Webby Junior?*

CURTIS WELLS (2/28/2010 4:07:06 PM): *he is fine, I think Joshua will like that nickname*

CURTIS WELLS (2/28/2010 4:07:12 PM): *it will sound like Spiderman to him*

LORIE.FINNIGHAN (2/28/2010 4:07:27 PM): *I am glad to hear he is fine. How old is he?*

CURTIS WELLS (2/28/2010 4:08:19 PM): *he is 6, will be 7 by April 25th*

LORIE.FINNIGHAN (2/28/2010 4:08:40 PM): *You took him with you?*

CURTIS WELLS (2/28/2010 4:09:15 PM): *yes he is with me, I*

won't let Joshua be all by himself

CURTIS WELLS (2/28/2010 4:09:29 PM): *I don't want Webby Jnr. to be out of my side*

LORIE.FINNIGHAN (2/28/2010 4:09:32 PM): *at his age, I surely hope not*

LORIE.FINNIGHAN (2/28/2010 4:10:01 PM): *well if he is the adventure action type of guy his dad seems to be, I guess, you doing the right thing*

LORIE.FINNIGHAN (2/28/2010 4:10:16 PM): *and what about Mocha?*

CURTIS WELLS (2/28/2010 4:10:57 PM): *Mocha is with the vet and I just miss him every time I read about your dogs*

CURTIS WELLS (2/28/2010 4:11:05 PM): *and yes, Joshua is the adventure type of guy*

LORIE.FINNIGHAN (2/28/2010 4:11:21 PM): *your vet dog sit for you? Nice Vet*

CURTIS WELLS (2/28/2010 4:11:40 PM): *yes*

LORIE.FINNIGHAN (2/28/2010 4:12:35 PM): *if I may ask, how come you got custody of the little guy?*

CURTIS WELLS (2/28/2010 4:13:17 PM): *my ex didn't want him, she actually didn't want the pregnancy; you know it was like I started too late*

LORIE.FINNIGHAN (2/28/2010 4:13:45 PM): *not sure what you mean?*

LORIE.FINNIGHAN (2/28/2010 4:14:01 PM): *so he never gets to see his Mum?*

CURTIS WELLS (2/28/2010 4:15:06 PM): *about 2 yrs now, we haven't seen her*

CURTIS WELLS (2/28/2010 4:15:15 PM): *she is like totally out of his life and mine*

CURTIS WELLS (2/28/2010 4:16:28 PM): *she moved on with her new man*

LORIE.FINNIGHAN (2/28/2010 4:16:53 PM): *that is something all right...so when are the Webby's getting back to Munich exactly?*

CURTIS WELLS (2/28/2010 4:20:18 PM): *next month certainly*

CURTIS WELLS (2/28/2010 4:20:25 PM): *oh! Next month is tomorrow lol*

LORIE.FINNIGHAN (2/28/2010 4:22:20 PM): *yes it is...look, you are obviously watching something on tele or playing Play Station games with your son and I need to go and walk my Lady, will be online later on?*
CURTIS WELLS (2/28/2010 4:24:08 PM): *okay take care of yourself okay...*
CURTIS WELLS (2/28/2010 4:24:14 PM): *looking forward to chatting more with you*
CURTIS WELLS (2/28/2010 4:29:46 PM): *have a good day with your little ones okay*

Lorie was well aware that she had asked him some of those questions before, but she wanted to check if he would be consistent with his answers, which he was.

She grabbed her jacket and called out to Lady. As she had promised Curtis to help him out, she decided that she would go to the airport and send him the cash that very afternoon, as she would not have another chance during the week, but, before she would go through with the transaction, she would make a little detour first.

She keyed the address that Curtis had given her in her GPS and drove off. Bertglen resembled very much any other small Bavarian village, with its country feel and farms all around. Although it seemed that it was a little bigger than her village, there were not many people around. Her GPS indicated to her that her destination would be two hundred metres to the right. She parked her car along the deserted street and decided to walk the rest of the way with her little dog.

* * *

After she got home, she quickly fed Lady and ran down to her office. As she opened her email box, she saw that, whilst she had been out, Curtis had written her an email in answer to her earlier note that day.

From: curtiswells62@xxxxxx
To: Lorie.finnighan@xxxxxx
Subject: Western Union
Date: Sunday, February 28. 2010, 02:44pm

Hello, Lorie,

How are you doing; I really do not know anything about the scam going on. I guess I need to be careful myself, then, since I am here already...

It will be good if you send in USD, 'cos I believe they have more of that in circulation here than EUR, but, all the same, whichever is good for you; I will be able to receive it.

I certainly understand why you should feel the way you feel with what the woman said to you; everyone has to be careful now, but certainly you know if I was a crook I wouldn't be giving out my details to you, and I want to assure you that you aren't losing your money.

Hope to hear from you soon and wish we could get to talk on the phone. I would love to hear your voice; say hi to your dogs for me, lol. I would one day love to meet them; I like pets a lot.

Hugs,
Curtis

She just did not know what to think anymore, but she was extremely upset with what she had discovered in Bertglen, and she was not going to hold back her discovery from Curtis, but, on the contrary, confront him with it, and what was with the hugs in his email, anyway? *What a joker,* she thought.

From: loriefinnighan@xxxxxx
To: curtiswells62@xxxxxx
Re: Western Union
Date Sunday, February 28.2010 6.17pm

Hoy! W,

Are you having me on or what? Before going to the airport, I decided to go with Lady for a little walk and a drive to... Berglern, and, funny enough, Number 45 was just a field. Can you help me out here? Thing is, if I had been satisfied, I would have stopped at the airport on my way back to send the cash to you.

What can I say, a part of me wants to trust you, but the other part tells me not to let my good heart get the better of me again.

It would be really unfair to you if you were really genuine and ended up being the one getting the hard treatment from me, not because I want to do it, but because I have been seriously let down in the past by putting faith in people.

Furthermore, and letting my guard down a little, like I have shared via messenger, I would like nothing more than if I could find that special friend in you.

So, help me out here, please.

If I could, I wish I could give you a big hug right now.

Lorie.

Before pressing the 'send' button, she read the email again and was satisfied with her approach, basically putting his back against the wall by letting him know that she had caught him red handed, in a way, but, on the other hand, extending back the hug to him as a signal that she had not shut the doors on him as she had done on Chuck Davis.

She spent the evening hovering around the house with her mind miles away from what she was really doing, totally and utterly confused as to why this man would provide her with what appeared to be a false address, which he knew was in the area where she lived. In her mind, either he was a complete idiot or a total risk taker. Not being able to shift her thoughts to anything else, let alone bring herself to go to bed, she decided to check her emails, and found a response from Curtis.

From: curtiswells@xxxxxx
To: loriefinnighan@xxxxxx
Subject: Western Union
Date: Sunday February 28, 2010 08:53pm

Hello, dearie,

There must have been a mistake there... Well, sometimes it can be inferred as 45a. I am sorry for the confusion; really, I understand that you have to be cautious with your money... I would react same way, too. I just hope you can trust me, 'cos I am not trying to hurt you, and I am really interested in the friendship, as well.
    Thanks for the email, anyway.
    If you are online, we will talk, okay.

Curtis.

The email did not quite satisfy her, but she saw it as a good sign that he had replied so quickly and that he wanted to talk, so she opened her messenger and saw that he was still online.

CURTIS WELLS (2/28/2010 9:14:52 PM): *I got your mail baby, I am sorry dearie... you know I am still trying to understand that place*
CURTIS WELLS (2/28/2010 9:14:56 PM): *moved there last Nov*
LORIE.FINNIGHAN (2/28/2010 9:15:22 PM): *Curtis, going through with this is going against my nature*
LORIE.FINNIGHAN (2/28/2010 9:15:49 PM): *I felt like I was*

kind of spying on you and I do not like that feeling at all

CURTIS WELLS (2/28/2010 9:16:02 PM): *I know how that feels*

CURTIS WELLS (2/28/2010 9:16:08 PM): *really it is not easy, I understand*

CURTIS WELLS (2/28/2010 9:16:16 PM): *but I hope you will try and trust me*

LORIE.FINNIGHAN (2/28/2010 9:16:49 PM): *but I need to know you are genuine...I do not let people close to me anymore, and maybe I will tell you why one day*

CURTIS WELLS (2/28/2010 9:17:20 PM): *I am very very genuine and wish there was another way to prove that to you*

LORIE.FINNIGHAN (2/28/2010 9:18:18 PM): *You are killing me, Webby*

CURTIS WELLS (2/28/2010 9:18:41 PM): *I wish I was there with you, to give you a hug*

LORIE.FINNIGHAN (2/28/2010 9:19:02 PM): *I want to trust you and I don't want to like you yet but for some reason, I already do...*

Lorie had a hard time controlling her emotions as she was having this conversation. Standing in front of that field had felt like a knife planted in her heart. She knew deep down how much she wanted to know this man more, and felt quite attracted to him, but, despite their emails and conversation, Curtis was still a total mystery to her and maybe that was where her fascination for him came from.

CURTIS WELLS (2/28/2010 9:19:38 PM): *same here too*

LORIE.FINNIGHAN (2/28/2010 9:20:01 PM): *what do you mean? You are having trust issues with me too*

Lorie knew immediately what he was referring to, but she did not really want to go down that path with him; not yet, anyway.

CURTIS WELLS (2/28/2010 9:20:17 PM): *liking you already*

CURTIS WELLS (2/28/2010 9:20:53 PM): *I know few about you, and you are an open person like me, so I do not see any reason why I should have trust issues with you*

LORIE.FINNIGHAN (2/28/2010 9:22:08 PM): *well, let say that I like to keep life as simple as possible*

LORIE.FINNIGHAN (2/28/2010 9:22:48 PM): *so I have no issues if you have some doubts as well*

CURTIS WELLS (2/28/2010 9:23:26 PM): *oh really nope, I am fine*

CURTIS WELLS (2/28/2010 9:23:31 PM): *how is Baberuth*

LORIE.FINNIGHAN (2/28/2010 9:24:28 PM): *I guess is fine. He is a regular at the pension. They love him so I am not worried. I just miss him. Not having my big guy around makes the house feels empty*

LORIE.FINNIGHAN (2/28/2010 9:25:02 PM): *and Lady is sad too, she just does not want to leave my bed. Looking for comforting I guess*

Aren't we all, she thought!

CURTIS WELLS (2/28/2010 9:26:16 PM): *how long are you going to miss him?*

LORIE.FINNIGHAN (2/28/2010 9:28:29 PM): *not sure, could take few more days... I am not familiar with this at all. It kind of reminds me this time when Baberuth was in love and my daughter turned around to him and said, Yes, Baberuth, I know, loves hurts...She was 15*

CURTIS WELLS (2/28/2010 9:28:53 PM): *where is your daughter now?*

LORIE.FINNIGHAN (2/28/2010 9:29:08 PM): *in the UK, she is at uni*

CURTIS WELLS (2/28/2010 9:30:41 PM): *wow that is nice*

LORIE.FINNIGHAN (2/28/2010 9:29:43 PM): *Look, I need to go to bed now so when do you need the money by exactly?*

CURTIS WELLS (2/28/2010 9:30:34 PM): *when are you going to be able to send it?*

CURTIS WELLS (2/28/2010 9:30:56 PM): *how old is your daughter?*

LORIE.FINNIGHAN (2/28/2010 9:31:11 PM): *she will be 20 in June*

Lorie decided deliberately to ignore the question about when she would be sending the cash, as she needed more time to think about it.

LORIE.FINNIGHAN (2/28/2010 9:31:27 PM): *that makes me feel old*

CURTIS WELLS (2/28/2010 9:31:28 PM): *wow that is cool, never see a picture of her... can you send me one*

LORIE.FINNIGHAN (2/28/2010 9:32:11 PM): *I have never sent you the proverbial Finnighan family picture?*

CURTIS WELLS (2/28/2010 9:32:25 PM): *yes you haven't*

LORIE.FINNIGHAN14 (2/28/2010 9:33:15 PM): *you mean no, I guess, hang on, coming right up but do you also have a picture of Webby Jnr. and Mocha?*

CURTIS WELLS (2/28/2010 9:35:53 PM): *I do not have a picture of Mocha but I do have a picture of Webby Jnr.*

LORIE.FINNIGHAN (2/28/2010 9:36:05 PM): *I have emailed it to you...Can I see it?*

CURTIS WELLS (2/28/2010 9:37:11 PM): *I will send it now*

LORIE.FINNIGHAN (2/28/2010 9:37:32 PM): *When are you coming back exactly? This is not a spying question, but I am just curious about you, that's all*

CURTIS WELLS (2/28/2010 9:38:22 PM): *our return date is 18th Thursday Mar*

CURTIS WELLS (2/28/2010 9:38:45 PM): *got it*

LORIE.FINNIGHAN (2/28/2010 9:39:47 PM): *okay...we still have a little bit of time I guess*

CURTIS WELLS (2/28/2010 9:41:32 PM): *your daughter is very pretty*

LORIE.FINNIGHAN (2/28/2010 9:42:06 PM): *Down Boy... she is my daughter... I was offered 2000 camels for her in Egypt*

CURTIS WELLS (2/28/2010 9:42:20 PM): *lol*

CURTIS WELLS (2/28/2010 9:42:37 PM): *just like her mom, they both have pretty eyes and the dogs are very cute*

CURTIS WELLS (2/28/2010 9:42:42 PM): *I will love to meet this family*

LORIE.FINNIGHAN (2/28/2010 9:42:56 PM): *well I guess, it is up to you*

CURTIS WELLS (2/28/2010 9:43:13 PM): *I want to in fact*

LORIE.FINNIGHAN (2/28/2010 9:43:18 PM): *where's the picture of that handsome guy of yours then*

CURTIS WELLS (2/28/2010 9:43:26 PM): *sent*

LORIE.FINNIGHAN14 (2/28/2010 9:44:14 PM): *You guys are so handsome... why are you doing this to me?*

LORIE.FINNIGHAN (2/28/2010 9:44:25 PM): *like I said, I don't want to like you yet*

CURTIS WELLS (2/28/2010 9:44:30 PM): *what Lorie*

CURTIS WELLS (2/28/2010 9:44:39 PM): *okay don't like me yet*

LORIE.FINNIGHAN (2/28/2010 9:45:05 PM): *give the girl a break!!! I know how Lady feels right now*

LORIE.FINNIGHAN (2/28/2010 9:45:52 PM): *she was seeing this good-looking golden retriever parading in front of her and she was not allowed to play... get the picture*

CURTIS WELLS (2/28/2010 9:49:07 PM): *yes I do*

CURTIS WELLS (2/28/2010 9:49:28 PM): *they are very sensitive dogs and think like humans*

CURTIS WELLS (2/28/2010 9:50:00 PM): *Mocha was not happy when we were travelling*

CURTIS WELLS (2/28/2010 9:50:06 PM): *I miss him so much*

LORIE.FINNIGHAN (2/28/2010 9:50:46 PM): *Yes, indeed, but at least with them, you know the deal... their expectations are clear .I want to go for my walk, my dinner and some cuddles and in return, they give you unconditional love*

CURTIS WELLS (2/28/2010 9:52:28 PM): *okay, you have to go now...*

LORIE.FINNIGHAN (2/28/2010 9:52:42 PM): *Okay, Hot Stuff, I need to really go to bed in order to be fresh to face my demons in the office tomorrow so have a good evening. A big hug to Webby Jnr... And BTW, I don't like you*

CURTIS WELLS (2/28/2010 9:53:23 PM): *okay*

Lorie shut down her laptop, not quite understanding what had just happened there, but something had. She took herself up to her bedroom feeling somewhat light on her feet, excited, even.

IV

Happy Easter

1

My Heart Goes Boom, Boom, Boom

Lorie's work situation was not getting any better. She was still confronted each day with the Berlin Wall raised between her and her team, despite her best efforts to establish a connection with the three people in her group. This was causing her more and more stress, and she was at a loss about how on earth she was going to resolve the situation. It was clear that they were challenging her silently. As she said to her boss, who said that the cold war was over! The cold war was alive and kicking right here in her department.

After yet again another day of enduring the harsh treatment imposed on her by her team, she took the opportunity of them having left for the day to sit back in her chair, and decided to seek some means of comfort somewhere else.

From: loriefinnighan@xxxxxx
To: curtiswells62@xxxxxx
Re: Hi
Date: Monday, March 1. 2010 5pm

Hi, Baby,

I am still in the office. Will you be online tonight?

Thanks,
Lorie.

After the weekly management meeting, Lorie drove home with a brick in her stomach thinking that something needed to change with her job or she would have to change the job again, a prospect that she was not quite ready to entertain at that particular moment.

She had lots of work to get through that night, so, on her way back, she opted to go through Burger King drive through and grabbed a burger, which she would eat on the drive back in order not to waste time having to organise food for herself after she got home.

After attending to her two stomachs on legs, she went up to wash her face, put her Nikky suit on and, after grabbing a drink from the kitchen, went to her office.

As she booted up her laptop, she got greeted by Curtis, who was obviously online.

CURTIS WELLS (3/2/2010 8:37:43 PM): *Hey babe*
FINNIGHAN.FINNIGHAN (3/2/2010 8:37:53 PM): *Hi Big Guy!*

Lorie had noticed that, in his most recent communications, Curtis had starting to refer to her in a more endearing way, calling her babe and dearie.

She just went along with it as, even if there was no substance behind those words, she would enjoy it for whatever it was.

LORIE.FINNIGHAN (3/2/2010 8:38:01 PM): *was just thinking about you*
CURTIS WELLS (3/2/2010 8:38:27 PM): *really...*

CURTIS WELLS (3/2/2010 8:38:32 PM): *I was thinking about you too*

LORIE.FINNIGHAN (3/2/2010 8:39:31 PM): *and why is were you thinking about me*

CURTIS WELLS (3/2/2010 8:39:59 PM): *I just thought what spending time with you will be like*

LORIE.FINNIGHAN (3/2/2010 8:40:17 PM): *hmmm interesting...why is that?*

CURTIS WELLS (3/2/2010 8:40:48 PM): *still trying to know the kind of feelings I am having*

LORIE.FINNIGHAN (3/2/2010 8:41:07 PM): *yep. I guess, I do feel a little disturbed as well*

LORIE.FINNIGHAN (3/2/2010 8:41:17 PM): *strange*

This conversation was definitely heading in a direction that she had not anticipated and, to add insult to injury, in the background, a song was playing, going, 'my heart goes boom, boom, boom every time I think of you'. It felt like entrapment, to her.

Lorie had recognised in herself that her mind had been on Curtis a lot more recently and in a way that was making her uncomfortable, so the very fact that Curtis told her that he had also, in a way, started to question his feelings for her destabilised her quite a bit, but, as she was not ready to let him know how disturbed she felt by him, she decided instead to put the ball back in his court:

LORIE.FINNIGHAN (3/2/2010 8:42:40 PM): *oy! share...*

CURTIS WELLS (3/2/2010 8:48:54 PM): *are you scared of falling in love*

Well, that was a very direct question, she thought. She did not really know how to deal with it, as she had not been accustomed to hearing guys referring to love and the falling in love thing in such a way. Her late husband was not, to say the least, the type of guy to discuss love feelings; in fact, the man was purely incapable of displaying any sign of affection, let alone romance. Lorie had, over the years, accepted him for the way he was, and not only did she not really give it much thought, but she would also accept any little gesture coming from him as being his call to romance. When she would relate the story on how he got her a rubber plant as a tenth wedding anniversary present from the minimarket on their way back from work, people would be absolutely outraged by the coldness of the gesture. She just would say, "That is just the way he is; I am not bothered, really, and, actually, I think it is quite funny."

In fact, over the years, Lorie had grown used to the idea of never receiving presents or flowers from her husband; he just was not the type.

Dwelling for a few a minute, also, on Curtis' direct question, she tiptoed her answer back to him.

LORIE.FINNIGHAN (3/2/2010 8:49:20 PM): *maybe, are you?*

As a couple of minutes had elapsed with no reply, she decided to push him a little more.

LORIE.FINNIGHAN (3/2/2010 8:52:05 PM): *cough up Webby...*
CURTIS WELLS (3/2/2010 8:53:43 PM): *lol maybe too*

From his light-hearted answer, she read that he had really not given the subject any real thought, either, until that very moment.

LORIE.FINNIGHAN (3/2/2010 8:55:52 PM): *you know...I am not sure if I am prepared to share this with you but I have learnt that when the L. demon knocks at your door, you cannot run away no matter how thick that door is*
LORIE.FINNIGHAN (3/2/2010 8:56:19 PM): *and it hits you when you are not looking*

CURTIS WELLS (3/2/2010 8:59:56 PM): *yes I read that too*

CURTIS WELLS (3/2/2010 9:00:23 PM): *when cupid calls it is very hard for one to run away*

LORIE.FINNIGHAN (3/2/2010 9:01:09 PM): *I am looking away, Babe but I am picking up some very strong vibes from you and I DON'T LIKE IT*

Lorie had the ability to sense people, even from a distance, at times; it had proven to be a valuable gift, but, in others, it was more of a curse than anything else. With Curtis, from the very first time she had seen him popping up on messenger, she had felt a current of electricity running through her. She knew then that the man was special, but she had no idea how and why.

She was not going to allow herself to admit the fact that she liked the idea of him and what she felt inside when she thought about him; in fact, she was going to block it out as, in her views, experiencing such feelings for someone whom she had never met was purely irrational. How could a few messages or emails possibly connect two human beings without them having had any human contact at all? That was pure nonsense, as far as she was concerned.

Curtis obviously got puzzled by the way she was reacting to the situation.

CURTIS WELLS (3/2/2010 9:02:03 PM): *why don't you like it?*

LORIE.FINNIGHAN (3/2/2010 9:02:23 PM): *for 2 reasons...*

LORIE.FINNIGHAN (3/2/2010 9:03:31 PM): *reason 1 is if I let the feelings take over, it would be hard to find out that when we finally meet, there is no chemistry.*

LORIE.FINNIGHAN (3/2/2010 9:04:18 PM): *reason number 2*

LORIE.FINNIGHAN (3/2/2010 9:04:21 PM): *forgot*

Lorie did not want to tell him that, in fact, she was already falling in love with him and that she enjoyed that feeling very much. She felt that would expose her way too much, too quickly.

CURTIS WELLS (3/2/2010 9:05:02 PM): *hmmm*
LORIE.FINNIGHAN (3/2/2010 9:05:09 PM): *what hmmm*
LORIE.FINNIGHAN (3/2/2010 9:06:17 PM): *something happened to me, W, 4 years ago and I am getting a sense of déjà vu except this time the situations are different.*

2

What About the Plan

Whilst at Inspect, Lorie had let someone get close to her and got involved with her work colleague way beyond what she could have predicted at the time. The two of them worked extremely close together and were more or less joints at the hips in the office. She enjoyed the close interaction and, at the time, felt really secure with this guy, as he was without a doubt Mr. Family Man, capital letters and all. However, over time, she had picked up on the fact that this man seemed to have some issues that she would not have initially associated with his home life. As the months had gone by, what was just initially a strong work friendship developed into a full-blown affair that went on for about eighteen months. Going through this had been, for her, nothing more than a giant roller coaster of emotions, as if on one hand she had recognised that this man needed his family and would never take the jump of leaving them; on the other hand, she resented the fact that, over time, she had developed some emotional dependency on him. After the merger, they both went their separate ways and, although they had kept contact for a while after, they never saw each other again. Based on what she had experienced back then, Lorie had grown even more protective of herself and, for her, the key to remain in control of her life was not to allow herself emotional dependency on anyone. As the conversation with Curtis was developing, she made a point of reminding herself of that rule she had imposed on herself. However, she was totally aware that the man was disturbing her and she needed to face it one way or the other.

LORIE.FINNIGHAN (3/2/2010 9:07:02 PM): *I am sensing some strong vibes from you and this is scary, Curtis*

CURTIS WELLS (3/2/2010 9:08:14 PM): *well let's just leave it like this and then when we meet we will see what it will be like*

LORIE.FINNIGHAN (3/2/2010 9:09:02 PM): *you make perfect sense. roll on March 18th, the suspense is killing me right now*

LORIE.FINNIGHAN (3/2/2010 9:09:58 PM): *I am sure you have been sent my way to torture me. anyway*

Lorie felt relieved that Curtis, unlike Chuck Davies, was not pushing her to admit her feelings, and his suggestion to just leave it the way it was for now was very welcomed by her. She decided to bring the conversation back to more grounded topics.

LORIE.FINNIGHAN (3/2/2010 9:10:28 PM): *when do you need your cash...I am working 8 till 10 except when I am chatting with you...can you hold on until the weekend*

LORIE.FINNIGHAN (3/2/2010 9:11:03 PM): *do you have a phone number where I could call you*

CURTIS WELLS (3/2/2010 9:11:23 PM): *I think I can do that, I am trying to get a cell here this week so we can sure talk*

LORIE.FINNIGHAN (3/2/2010 9:11:53 PM): *you don't have a phone at your apartment?*

LORIE.FINNIGHAN (3/2/2010 9:12:18 PM): *hey, how did you get to live in Germany?*

CURTIS WELLS (3/2/2010 9:12:48 PM): *you asking because of*

the language problem right

CURTIS WELLS (3/2/2010 9:12:57 PM): *well still coping and Germans are very nice*

CURTIS WELLS (3/2/2010 9:13:08 PM): *I wanted to leave the US life and raise my son European*

LORIE.FINNIGHAN (3/2/2010 9:13:29 PM): *I see*

LORIE.FINNIGHAN (3/2/2010 9:13:48 PM): *funny...my husband and I wanted to retire to Florida*

CURTIS WELLS (3/2/2010 9:14:05 PM): *really*

CURTIS WELLS (3/2/2010 9:14:12 PM): *Florida is a nice place too*

LORIE.FINNIGHAN (3/2/2010 9:14:13 PM): *Yep*

LORIE.FINNIGHAN (3/2/2010 9:14:27 PM): *we used to go for 2 weeks holidays every year*

LORIE.FINNIGHAN (3/2/2010 9:15:08 PM): *and we had this little place on the east coast, off the beaten tourist track, which was like a sanctuary*

CURTIS WELLS (3/2/2010 9:15:21 PM): *lol*

FINNIGHAN.FINNIGHAN (3/2/2010 9:15:43 PM): *totally peaceful, a 2 police car town where everyone was over 60*

FINNIGHAN.FINNIGHAN (3/2/2010 9:15:51 PM): *even the police officers*

FINNIGHAN.FINNIGHAN (3/2/2010 9:16:01 PM): *and they used to have disco nights every Saturday*

FINNIGHAN.FINNIGHAN (3/2/2010 9:16:25 PM): *but why Germany?*

Curtis wells (3/2/2010 9:18:28 PM): yes it is very peaceful

Curtis wells (3/2/2010 9:18:35 PM): but I want the European life

LORIE.FINNIGHAN (3/2/2010 9:19:27 PM): *well, I will admit that I do love it here and I have lived in several countries*

LORIE..FINNIGHAN (3/2/2010 9:19:50 PM): *do you speak German?*

CURTIS WELLS (3/2/2010 9:23:43 PM): *nope*

LORIE.FINNIGHAN (3/2/2010 9:24:03 PM): *me neither... great... perfect team*

CURTIS WELLS (3/2/2010 9:24:19 PM): *yes right*

CURTIS WELLS (3/2/2010 9:24:51 PM): *you don't talk much*

about your husband

CURTIS WELLS (3/2/2010 9:24:58 PM): *wanna tell me about you guys*

LORIE.FINNIGHAN (3/2/2010 9:25:21 PM): *he was English. still is I suppose*

LORIE.FINNIGHAN (3/2/2010 9:25:34 PM): *we were married 16 years*

CURTIS WELLS (3/2/2010 9:25:55 PM): *do you like soccer, I am watching Ireland vs. Brazil, a friendly match*

CURTIS WELLS (3/2/2010 9:26:15 PM): *wow I was married for 13 yrs before the divorce with my ex*

LORIE.FINNIGHAN (3/2/2010 9:27:00 PM): *No I don't like soccer but if you were watching this match here right now, I would massage your shoulder and back to make it even more relaxing*

CURTIS WELLS (3/2/2010 9:27:53 PM): *hmm that is really good then*

LORIE.FINNIGHAN (3/2/2010 9:29:01 PM): *well one has to leverage on all the opportunities, right? you watching football does not mean that I need to miss out on you, right*

CURTIS WELLS (3/2/2010 9:30:07 PM): *yes you are right, now I really want the massage*

LORIE.FINNIGHAN (3/2/2010 9:30:30 PM): *and guess what. I am really GOOD*

CURTIS WELLS (3/2/2010 9:31:13 PM): *now you are making me want....*

LORIE.FINNIGHAN (3/2/2010 9:31:22 PM): *?*

LORIE.FINNIGHAN (3/2/2010 9:31:31 PM): *what did you say?*

LORIE.FINNIGHAN (3/2/2010 9:32:15 PM): *I just love the feel of a strong man..*

CURTIS WELLS (3/2/2010 9:34:30 PM): *me too I love that*

CURTIS WELLS (3/2/2010 9:34:33 PM): *what are you doing?*

LORIE.FINNIGHAN (3/2/2010 9:34:55 PM): *the feel of a strong man??? are you gay???*

CURTIS WELLS (3/2/2010 9:35:52 PM): *lol I was expecting you to ask that lol, I am not gay... just love being the strong man*

LORIE.FINNIGHAN (3/2/2010 9:36:12 PM): *really!! now you are teasing me... not nice, Webby*
CURTIS WELLS (3/2/2010 9:42:41 PM): *lol*
CURTIS WELLS (3/2/2010 9:42:53 PM): *you know I am beginning to like Webby*

It was obvious that there was some relief felt by the two of them, as their conversation got a little less serious and more playful. Lorie enjoyed teasing people around her and she did not need much encouragement to start messing about, a little to test how he would handle her playfulness.

LORIE.FINNIGHAN (3/2/2010 9:45:18 PM): *do you know him?*
LORIE.FINNIGHAN (3/2/2010 9:45:30 PM): *do you want me to tell you about him?*
CURTIS WELLS (3/2/2010 9:45:35 PM): *sure*

Apparently, guys were constantly starved for appreciation, and needed to be told and reminded how wonderful and special they were on a very regular basis. Or so she had read in some woman's magazine at her hairdresser one day.

She decided that she would put that theory to test right there and then.

LORIE.FINNIGHAN (3/2/2010 9:46:35 PM): *well, he is this guy, who is drop dead gorgeous*
LORIE.FINNIGHAN (3/2/2010 9:46:49 PM): *he is obviously a strong man*
LORIE.FINNIGHAN (3/2/2010 9:46:52 PM): *intelligent*
LORIE.FINNIGHAN (3/2/2010 9:46:57 PM): *ambitious*
LORIE.FINNIGHAN (3/2/2010 9:47:01 PM): *successful*
LORIEN.FINNIGHAN (3/2/2010 9:47:18 PM): *no doubt can charm the pants off any women*
LORIE.FINNIGHAN (3/2/2010 9:47:32 PM): *and big F... trouble for me*
CURTIS WELLS (3/2/2010 9:48:34 PM): *now I am laughing*

hard

LORIE.FINNIGHAN (3/2/2010 9:48:54 PM): *good keep doing it big guy*

LORIE.FINNIGHAN (3/2/2010 9:49:33 PM): *and what is so funny exactly... you know this guy?*

CURTIS WELLS (3/2/2010 9:50:04 PM): *charm the pants of any woman, is making me laugh 'cos I never knew I could do that*

LORIE.FINNIGHAN (3/2/2010 9:50:31 PM): *oh, Curtis, don't be so humble. I am not buying it*

Lorie had studied the picture that Curtis had sent her quite hard, and she did not believe one bit that he pretended not knowing that his somewhat angel baby face did not have any effect on women; in fact, she truly believed that he used his charming skills in a very manipulative way.

LORIE.FINNIGHAN (3/2/2010 9:50:43 PM): *I know your type*

CURTIS WELLS (3/2/2010 9:53:21 PM): *I am speechless*

FINNIGHAN.FINNIGHAN14 (3/2/2010 9:53:44 PM): *caught with its hands in the cookie jar, is he?*

CURTIS WELLS (3/2/2010 9:55:11 PM): *nope he is not*

As the man seemed to be game, she decided to escalate her banter a notch.

LORIE.FINNIGHAN (3/2/2010 9:56:50 PM): *do you want to know what goes through my head when I think of you?*

CURTIS WELLS (3/2/2010 9:57:28 PM): *sure*

LORIE.FINNIGHAN (3/2/2010 9:57:42 PM): *hmmm, can you handle it?*

CURTIS WELLS (3/2/2010 10:00:51 PM): *YES*

Time to go for the kill, she thought.

LORIE.FINNIGHAN (3/2/2010 10:01:18 PM): *Fantastic Sex on*

the kitchen counter, the type that leaves you wanting more and more and more

CURTIS WELLS (3/2/2010 10:02:28 PM): *I guess our thoughts have been kinda going on the same direction*

LORIE.FINNIGHAN (3/2/2010 10:02:52 PM): *fantastic… it is your damn vibes, you know*

LORIE.FINNIGHAN (3/2/2010 10:03:29 PM): *what can I say, you are doing it for me Webby… STOP IT!*

CURTIS WELLS (3/2/2010 10:04:51 PM): *okay*

LORIE.FINNIGHAN (3/2/2010 10:04:59 PM): *OKAY?*

LORIE.FINNIGHAN (3/2/2010 10:05:17 PM): *you can't do that…*

LORIE.FINNIGHAN (3/2/2010 10:06:16 PM): *it has been a long time, you know. I am very sensitive right now*

Lorie selected an emoticon and added it to her conversation.

LORIE.FINNIGHAN (3/2/2010 10:07:17 PM): *damn wrong one… that is the one I wanted to send you*

Not really concentrating, she had sent Curtis the love emoticon when she had just wanted to send him a wink.

CURTIS WELLS (3/2/2010 10:07:31 PM): *haha*

CURTIS WELLS (3/2/2010 10:07:51 PM): *yea right wrong one*

LORIE.FINNIGHAN (3/2/2010 10:08:26 PM): *I don't do that girly stuff!*

LORIE.FINNIGHAN (3/2/2010 10:08:37 PM): *I am a grown, mature, woman, you know*

CURTIS WELLS (3/2/2010 10:09:43 PM): *yes I know that*

Curtis seemed to not quite know how to deal with her humour and redirected the conversation to more grounded, day to day, and more comfortable subjects:

CURTIS WELLS (3/2/2010 10:09:49 PM): *how is your Baberuth*

LORIE.FINNIGHAN (3/2/2010 10:10:22 PM): *still in his pension, missing him like hell*

LORIE.FINNIGHAN (3/2/2010 10:10:44 PM): *but I need to make sure that they are not in love anymore*

CURTIS WELLS (3/2/2010 10:11:10 PM): *why do you want to do that*

CURTIS WELLS (3/2/2010 10:11:18 PM): *it is bad to stop love babe*

LORIE.FINNIGHAN (3/2/2010 10:11:46 PM): *I don't want to stop it. life is too short, Babe!*

CURTIS WELLS (3/2/2010 10:14:48 PM): *good*

LORIE.FINNIGHAN (3/2/2010 10:15:51 PM): *I guess...what are your views on the subject/*

CURTIS WELLS (3/2/2010 10:16:32 PM): *well if it is healthy for both of them, fine... but they are your dogs so whatever you do fine*

LORIE.FINNIGHAN (3/2/2010 10:18:06 PM): *Lady is still a baby not ready to have babies and it is too painful to see them suffering. It is best to keep them apart until things are back to normal*

CURTIS WELLS (3/2/2010 10:18:36 PM): *I think you are right*

LORIE.FINNIGHAN (3/2/2010 10:18:38 PM): *as my daughter said once to Baberuth, loves hurts*

LORIE.FINNIGHAN (3/2/2010 10:19:25 PM): *where is your family?*

CURTIS WELLS (3/2/2010 10:19:40 PM): *I am the only child of my parent*

LORIE.FINNIGHAN (3/2/2010 10:20:03 PM): *me too*

CURTIS WELLS (3/2/2010 10:21:06 PM): *and I have lost both of my parents, though I do stay in touch with my cousins in Ireland*

LORIE.FINNIGHAN (3/2/2010 10:21:25 PM): *I like Ireland.*

LORIE.FINNIGHAN (3/2/2010 10:21:57 PM): *My dad is dead but my mum lives in France and we have a very big family*

LORIE.FINNIGHAN (3/2/2010 10:22:10 PM): *with lots of cousin and nephews*

LORIE.FINNIGHAN (3/2/2010 10:22:19 PM): *and nieces as well*

LORIE.FINNIGHAN (3/2/2010 10:22:22 PM): *we are very close*

CURTIS WELLS (3/2/2010 10:23:00 PM): *that is good, I will someday love to meet a large family 'cos I never had one*

LORIE.FINNIGHAN (3/2/2010 10:23:50 PM): *well don't get ahead of yourself but they are great and my husband adored going to visit as on his side they were not close*

CURTIS WELLS (3/2/2010 10:24:19 PM): *well I am sure you will help me get used to them*

LORIE.FINNIGHAN (3/2/2010 10:24:50 PM): *I also have some great friends who live in Paris, they more like family to me, they come 4 times a year to escape their own kids*

LORIE.FINNIGHAN (3/2/2010 10:25:03 PM): *do you have friends in Munich?*

LORIE.FINNIGHAN (3/2/2010 10:25:30 PM): *apart from all the women you are charming ?*

CURTIS WELLS (3/2/2010 10:26:04 PM): *well I don't know what they say in German... some just wink*

CURTIS WELLS (3/2/2010 10:26:11 PM): *I have people that I just talk to*

LORIE.FINNIGHAN (3/2/2010 10:27:20 PM): *what do you mean they wink? not on! but yes, I think I know what you mean*

LORIE.FINNIGHAN (3/2/2010 10:27:32 PM): *my life has not exactly been social friendly*

LORIE.FINNIGHAN (3/2/2010 10:27:53 PM): *I don't mind. I am not a crowd person*

LORIE.FINNIGHAN (3/2/2010 10:27:58 PM): *more a one on one*

CURTIS WELLS (3/2/2010 10:28:03 PM): *me too*

CURTIS WELLS (3/2/2010 10:29:26 PM): *so that is why I am looking for our one on one*

LORIE.FINNIGHAN (3/2/2010 10:29:40 PM): *you bet*

LORIE.FINNIGHAN (3/2/2010 10:30:00 PM): *what do you like to do when you are not working?*

CURTIS WELLS (3/2/2010 10:31:50 PM): *I like spending time with my son*

CURTIS WELLS (3/2/2010 10:33:12 PM): *we do a lot of things, play games, go out, just try to do anything fun*

LORIE.FINNIGHAN (3/2/2010 10:34:29 PM): *that is great,*

CURTIS WELLS (3/2/2010 10:35:04 PM): *do you see your daughter a lot*

LORIE.FINNIGHAN (3/2/2010 10:35:12 PM): *unfortunately no*

LORIE.FINNIGHAN (3/2/2010 10:35:42 PM): *she comes home for Xmas and the summer holidays unless we decide to meet up in France*

LORIE.FINNIGHAN (3/2/2010 10:36:00 PM): *I am not sure that she will make it to Munich this summer*

CURTIS WELLS (3/2/2010 10:36:21 PM): *oh that means you guys will meet in France*

LORIE.FINNIGHAN (3/2/2010 10:36:25 PM): *We are doing a big family party in France for her 20th*

LORIE.FINNIGHAN (3/2/2010 10:36:43 PM): *and then she is going to Australia to visit her uncle*

LORIE.FINNIGHAN (3/2/2010 10:36:58 PM): *her dad's brother*

LORIE.FINNIGHAN (3/2/2010 10:37:45 PM): *tell me, is Webby Jnr. at school yet?*

CURTIS WELLS (3/2/2010 10:39:08 PM): *Webby Jnr. is starting first grade*

LORIE.FINNIGHAN (3/2/2010 10:39:17 PM): *impressive!*

LORIE.FINNIGHAN (3/2/2010 10:39:26 PM): *is he going to German school?*

CURTIS WELLS (3/2/2010 10:39:36 PM): *yes I want him to do that*

CURTIS WELLS (3/2/2010 10:39:41 PM): *what do you think*

LORIE.FINNIGHAN (3/2/2010 10:40:12 PM): *well, I guess for the integration it is good as he will have friends who live in the neighbourhood*

CURTIS WELLS (3/2/2010 10:41:04 PM): *yes that is why I thought about it, for integration*

CURTIS WELLS (3/2/2010 10:43:06 PM): *Joshua is an early bloomer, he always gets home tutoring*

LORIE.FINNIGHAN (3/2/2010 10:43:32 PM): *you have to do what you feel is right for the little man, Curtis*

LORIE.FINNIGHAN (3/2/2010 10:44:00 PM): *but I would not have wanted to see Jane in their school; furthermore, I don't like the way they get them to think*

CURTIS WELLS (3/2/2010 10:45:31 PM): *well I have been evaluating the options and Joshua actually wants to go to an English school*

LORIE.FINNIGHAN (3/2/2010 10:45:59 PM): *just see how it is going and you can always change if it does not work*

LORIE.FINNIGHAN (3/2/2010 10:46:21 PM): *Jane went to the international school in the village and they did a great job with her*

LORIE.FINNIGHAN (3/2/2010 10:46:27 PM): *she misses it*

CURTIS WELLS (3/2/2010 10:46:34 PM): *you are right that is what I will do*

LORIE.FINNIGHAN (3/2/2010 10:47:19 PM): *Okay Babe, this girl needs to go and get her beauty sleep now and have steamy dreams of fantastic sex on the kitchen counter*

CURTIS WELLS (3/2/2010 10:50:21 PM): *okay dearie*

CURTIS WELLS (3/2/2010 10:50:33 PM): *I will talk to you tomorrow hopefully*

Agitated by the conversation, all she could do was to lie in her bed and stare at her ceiling. Fifteen minutes elapsed before she got up again and went back to her office to check if he was still online. He was.

LORIE.FINNIGHAN (3/2/2010 11:18:34 PM): *can't sleep... it is your fault! Curtis wells*

CURTIS WELLS (3/2/2010 11:19:49 PM): *just wish you were here*

LORIE.FINNIGHAN (3/2/2010 11:20:20 PM): *it is a bit like that... why, may I ask?*

CURTIS WELLS (3/2/2010 11:20:53 PM): *I don't know babe*

LORIE.FINNIGHAN (3/2/2010 11:21:29 PM): *what is going through your mind? I have opened a little bit too much for my own comfort, so match me*

CURTIS WELLS (3/2/2010 11:22:10 PM): *I want a woman feel*

LORIE.FINNIGHAN (3/2/2010 11:22:21 PM): *me too...*

LORIE.FINNIGHAN (3/2/2010 11:22:28 PM): *A man that is*

LORIE.FINNIGHAN (3/2/2010 11:23:01 PM): *Your touch 'cos, something tells me that it would feel wonderful*

LORIE.FINNIGHAN (3/2/2010 11:24:18 PM): *I sense that it would be warm, tender, and loving, making me feel totally secure*

CURTIS WELLS (3/2/2010 11:25:05 PM): *yes and it can make you lose guard*

LORIE.FINNIGHAN (3/2/2010 11:25:23 PM): *are you losing your guard?*

CURTIS WELLS (3/2/2010 11:25:37 PM): *lol*

LORIE.FINNIGHAN (3/2/2010 11:26:19 PM): *come on....don't be shy...I don't bite*

LORIE.FINNIGHAN (3/2/2010 11:28:17 PM): *what are you doing???????*

CURTIS WELLS (3/2/2010 11:29:33 PM): *nothing really, trying to sleep and then probably dream about you*

LORIE.FINNIGHAN (3/2/2010 11:30:05 PM): *you sleep with your computer?*

CURTIS WELLS (3/2/2010 11:31:51 PM): *I will turn it off if you leave*

CURTIS WELLS (3/2/2010 11:32:04 PM): *okay lets stop this, we planned not to go this far*

LORIE.FINNIGHAN (3/2/2010 11:33:08 PM): *F the plan! life is too short and for what its worth, imagine that I am with you, giving lots of tender kisses all over your beautiful body and I will do the same*

LORIE.FINNIGHAN (3/2/2010 11:33:51 PM): *we don't have to act on it when we see each other but there is nothing wrong with MSN sex, right? Gee what has a girl to do to get it these days..LOL...*

LORIE.FINNIGHAN (3/2/2010 11:34:07 PM): *if that girl was me of course, but I don't do that*

CURTIS WELLS (3/2/2010 11:34:47 PM): *thanks for telling me that*

CURTIS WELLS (3/2/2010 11:34:53 PM): *that just made my night*

CURTIS WELLS (3/2/2010 11:34:58 PM): *now I will sleep well*

LORIE.FINNIGHAN (3/2/2010 11:35:03 PM): *me too*

As they ended the conversation, Lorie felt rather at ease and somewhat at peace that Curtis was being genuine with her.

3

Kisses & Hugs

5:30 a.m. – Off went the alarm. Lorie came out of a very deep sleep. In fact, she had not slept so well for a very long time. She literally sailed through her morning routines and set off for work ahead of time.

Nothing could affect her on that day; she kept herself busy and totally blacked out the negative vibes that were flying around her in her office.

After her crew had cleared the building, she quickly checked her private emails and wrote a short one to Curtis.

To: curtiswells62@xxxxxx
From: loriefinnighan@xxxxxx
Ref: Are we watching soccer again tonight?
Date: Wednesday, March 23.4.54pm

Hi, Curtis,

I really enjoyed the game last night.

CU
L

After taking a short walk around the building to think about what she needed to do next, Lorie went back to her desk and just worked through without noticing the time running away. It was well past nine by the time she drove her car up the exit ramp of her office building. Due to the late hour, she opted for Burger King, which was conveniently placed on her way, ordered her usual, and drove home listening to her Enrique Iglesias CD. She would have never admitted in public, or under torture, for that matter, that she liked Enrique, so she kept her shameful secret confined in her car for the late-night drives.

As she got home, she found a message from Sophie on her answer phone; she wanted to know how things were going.

Good old, Sophie, thought Lorie, checking the time to see if it would be too late to call her back. With the UK being one hour behind her, Lorie picked up the phone and dialled Sophie's number.

"Hi, Sophie, got your message. Is this too late to talk?"

"Not at all; how are you doing, girl?" asked Sophie.

"Well, it is going. I cannot say that things are getting better with my evil crew, but I cannot say they are getting worse, so, for now, I can grin and bear it, I guess. So, what is new on your side, then?"

"Pretty much the usual. Those plunkers really do not have a clue about what they are doing," said Sophie. Sophie was referring to the new senior management team that had taken over since the merger. "Now, I am going to make you chuckle. Klaus called me this morning and asked me if I was interested in touching his three elements." Sophie could not stop laughing.

"He what? What did you say? No, thanks, they are not big enough for me?"

"Oh, don't! I could barely answer him as all I wanted to do was to burst laughing."

Sophie's new boss, Klaus, was part of the old German crew who had recently been promoted to take over the international software sales of the business. Sophie had despised the man long before his promotion, but having him as a boss was somewhat adding insult to injury, as far as she was concerned. Klaus had very little knowledge of international business and his English was extremely thin on the ground, which made communication difficult between him and Sophie.

The two women had worked for as many years as they could remember in a very international multi-culti environment and, over the years, the two friends had had great unforgivable moments as the so-called various nation stereotypes had proven to be not just stereotypes, but actually quite real. They had had priceless experiences of sitting in meetings with the strict and inflexible Germans, the loud, flamboyant Italians, the 'no risk takers' diplomatic English, the very special French and the wannabe world dominators, Americans. As the various characters would defend their own flags, all communicating in a language that was, for the most part, not their native one, the dynamic could get very spicy at times, with everyone, in essence, using the same language, but understanding something completely different.

"So, what did you say?" asked Lorie.

"I told him that I would think about it," she replied, still laughing.

"I must say that I do not envy you, really; so what do you intend to do?"

"Honestly, I wish I could just slap my resignation on his desk, but I do not want to leave unless I have something else secured first. And, as it so happens, one of my customers has approached me and asked me if I would be interested in coming on board full time working for them. I would still be doing what I am doing now, but sitting on the other side of the desk, so to speak," said Sophie.

"That is really good, Sophie," said Lorie.

"Yes and *no*. There is a glitch in the pipe work," added Sophie.

"Isn't there always? What is it?" enquired Lorie.

"It is one of my Norwegian clients, and I would have to relocate to Oslo."

"Ouch! How do you feel about that?"

"I am not really sure. It is a big step to take, but they have put quite a big envelope on the table," shared Sophie.

"Well, girl, I would not advise you one way or the other. It is a big decision and you need to weigh out the pros and cons seriously. All I can say to you is that I have spent most of my life relocating and country hopping, and if you decide to go through with this, you need to take the jump one hundred percent."

"What do you mean?"

"What I mean is that, if you are entertaining the idea of doing a Monday to Friday thing with going back home to the UK over the weekend or every other weekend, you are going to kill yourself physically, as you will be living in a suitcase, and you can kiss your social life goodbye. I am not trying to influence you, but I am just sharing with you my own experience," said Lorie.

"I appreciate you sharing your opinion with me, and yes, I was looking at going for the commuting option, as I do not want to give up my house in the UK and, furthermore, I have my mother to think of, as well. I will definitely give it some serious thought. Thanks, Lorie," said Sophie.

"Hey, moving on to a more serious subject, have I told you about my Internet quest for a rich husband?"

Sophie laughed. "What are you up to now?"

"Well, you know, we are not getting any younger and, whilst I was hunting for a new job, I thought I would start hunting for a rich husband before my bad looks disappear with age," said Lorie playfully.

"So, any good prospects?"

"Well, I have had some customers, but holy moley, Sarah, that is a long story for another time. The status now is that I have eliminated four of them and I am just pursuing one whom I am finding quite intriguing. I am not taking it too seriously, but he gives me a good distraction and we have good messenger chats."

"Oh, okay, that sounds interesting."

"For now, I am quite happy with the way things are. I am very sceptical about this Internet dating thing, but hey, he makes good company in the evening," said Lorie.

"Well, you are having the right approach, I guess. I know that it worked for quite few of my friends, but I understand where you are coming from," said Sophie.

"I better go now, as it is getting late. Speak to you really soon, Sophie, and if you just want to bounce off thoughts on your Norway prospects, I am happy to listen."

"Thanks, Lorie; have a good night."

As Lorie was really enjoying her conversation with Sophie, she had, in the process, lost sense of the time and was quite surprised to see how late it was.

Way too late to start engaging in a messenger conversation with Curtis, should he decide to pop up. She opted to send him a short email before taking herself up to bed.

From: loriefinighan@xxxxxx
To: curtiswells62@xxxxxx
Subject: Hi
Date: Wednesday, March 3 2010 10:13pm

Hi, Babe,

Sorry, we did not get to chat. I was quite looking forward to it.

I left the office well after 9:00 and still bashed at my laptop for over an hour after I got home... Who lives like that, really?

I hope I did not offend you too much with my forwardness last night.

Anyway, I hope you had a very enjoyable day today and that you are doing great business there.

I am going to bed now and hope that you will not trouble my sleep (please do; it is nice), but I don't like you, anyway.

Have a good one,
Lorie

PS: don't call me Dearie; it makes me feel like either an old lady or a dairy product; not sure which one...

Curtis had, on a few occasions, referred to her as 'dearie'. For some reason, she could not help but find the term to be a sign of patronising endearments. She decided to make a point of setting the record straight in a 'dearie' way.

The following morning, Lorie did not need the alarm to remind her that a new day had come and she needed to do it all over again. Get up, walk the dogs, go to work, cope with the unfriendly environment of her department, leave the office, stop at Burger King, feed the dogs, and back to bed. That particular morning, in fact, she decided to get ahead and see how fast she could fly through her very predictable day without incurring any injuries along the way.

To her delight, she found an email from Curtis in her mailbox, and concluded that he had probably logged on shortly after she had logged out.

To: Lorie.finnighan@xxxxxx
From: curtiswells62@xxxxxx
Re: Sorry, I did not get to catch you online
Date: Wednesday, March 3, 2010 11:41 pm

Hello, Sweetness,

I am sorry that we didn't meet each other online; I hope you did have a wonderful day. I miss you and it was nice thinking about you.

Kisses and hugs,
Curtis.

"Oh so, now we are moving on to kisses and hugs! How about that? *Hein, hein*," she exclaimed, but, despite her best efforts, she could not help herself but like it a little too much.

She quickly replied to his message and moved on with her morning routines.

To: curtiswells62@xxxxxx
From: loriefinnighan@xxxxxx
Re: Sorry, I did not get to catch you online
Date: Thursday, March 4, 2010, 5:13 AM

Hello, Trouble,

Likewise... maybe tonight, hein! But we must remember the plan, right?
Have a super duper day, Babe!

She was not quite ready to go as far as 'hugs and kisses'. Nevertheless, by addressing him as 'babe', she wanted to indicate to him that she was comfortable with slowly getting closer; if one can ever get close to another human being via email, that is.

She also made a point of reminding him of 'the plan'. During one of their long late-night messenger chats, they had agreed that, although they had found each other through an Internet dating website, they would keep their relationship on a friendly level until such time as Curtis was back from Nigeria and they could meet. However, during one of their most recent messenger exchanges, they had both got a little carried away with one another and shared that, that particular night, they had other plans in mind.

Lorie had enjoyed the shameful escalation of their conversation that night, but, at this stage, she did not want to start entertaining the idea that this cyber friendship could develop into something a little heavier before she had met the guy face to face After all, she did not want to run the risk of finding herself attached to this man only to discover further along the road that they had no real attraction for each other after meeting in person. *That would just be plain nasty, now, would it not,* she thought.

* * *

5:30 a.m. *Buzz! Buzz! Buzz!*

Lorie extended her arm towards the object of torture and killed it. She lay back for a little while staring at the ceiling whilst she was slowly getting her brain back into gear for yet another fun-packed day at the office. Baberuth was lying next to her snoring away, and looked as if he had a smile on his face. Lorie loved watching him sleeping; he always looked so peaceful, while, on the other hand, Lady did not seem to be familiar with the 'peaceful' concept, as she was jumping all over Lorie, relentlessly trying to scratch Lorie's hair with her paw.

* * *

Upon her return home that evening, Lorie was not really in the mood for food, so, after kicking off her work clothes, she quickly threw some Special K's in a bowl, poured out some cold milk over it, and ran downstairs to go through her emails and pay a couple of bills, which had been sitting on her desk for a week, as she just could not be bothered. Lorie spent over ten hours a day dealing with banks and money for her company; the last thing she wanted to do when she got home was to look at one more bank account, least of all hers, which always seemed like a disaster zone no matter how much money she made.

As she saw that she had a new email from Curtis in her mailbox, the bills got pushed aside.

From:curtiswell62@xxxxxx
To:loriefinnighan@xxxxxx
Subject:sorry I missed you online
Date:Thursday, March 4, 2010 5.57pm

Hello, L,

Funny you called me trouble; guess you will have to tell me why; anyway, I will be looking forward to us getting to chat tonight and sure do remember the plan.

Missed you.
Curtis xoxo

4

The Game Is *On*

The game is on, she thought after reading the email. The man had requested a messenger date. *But what does 'xoxo' stands for, actually,* she asked herself.

She opened her messenger and, although Curtis was showing on offline status, she decided to put up a little daring welcoming message, which she knew would pop up on his screen when he next connected.

LORIEFINNIGHAN(3/5/2010 8:45:27 PM): *Oy, Lady Killer, fancy some some tender loving chat? I surely could use some myself*

That evening, she decided to do a little cleaning around her office, which she had disregarded for quite a while due to the time restraint she constantly felt under. Her week days were long and left her very little room, if any, to deal with her private life. The weekends were time like military operations, as they seemed to just flash in front of her before she had the time to think about it.

As she was going around her office picking up empty cups and glasses, which by magic, had multiplied in her absence, putting away folders she had taken out in a hurry during the week, as needing this or that piece of paper, sweeping and polishing the dresser, coffee table and TV, she was keeping, the whole time, an eye on her laptop screen to see if her messenger started flashing, letting her know that Curtis was online.

It became obvious that he would probably not log in that night, so Lorie decided to take the opportunity to answer him about her marital past, as Curtis had pointed out that she seemed to be keeping that part of her life pretty close to her chest.

From: loriefinnighan@Yahoo.com
To: curtiswells62@Yahoo.com
Subject: Lorie
Date: Friday, March 5, 2010, 9:16 PM

Fancy a tender, loving chat? I sure could use one myself, all truth be told... I guess you are having Daddy time with Webby Jnr. and so you should. You are a very dedicated father, Curtis Wells. That is really nice. Enjoy it whilst you can; they grow so fast.

When Jane left home to go to uni, it was as if I had just been hit by a bus when I dropped her at the airport. I was not ready to see her leave home and I had been living in denial all the months leading up to her departure. So enjoy your little boy, Curtis, as the good-looking kid he is; before you know it, he will be bringing home the girlfriends... Takes after his father, I guess.

You mentioned that I did not say much about my marriage, so maybe, since we cannot chat tonight, I should take this time to write to you about it; it will save us some precious time on messenger. As I had mentioned to you before, we were married for sixteen years. It was by no means a bed of roses, trust me. I guess we had your typical run of the mill marriage story. Married young and life took its toll between jobs and having a child; we grew apart romantically, if I can put it that way. We got along okay, but it was more a partnership than a relationship. And you and I have something in common when it comes to our marriages; both of our partners outsourced their affections elsewhere. I tend to say that my husband joined the navy, if you know what I mean. He travelled quite a lot with his job and always seemed to have someone to go to. I did not mind; I did not have those kinds of feelings anymore for him, really. I am not blaming him in any way; I guess both parties made their own mistakes. Live and learn, Curtis... that is what life is about, right?

We loved each other, but we just did not know how to love each other, if that makes any sense to you. I am a very affectionate person. I need to give affection as much as I need to receive it. My husband just was not and I had kind of learnt to live without it. But I want to catch up on all the hugs, cuddles, affectionate and passionate love making that I have missed out on all these years. We are not getting any younger, are we, Curtis, so, for me, I want to take whatever I can whilst I still can.

I knew about his little escapades, but I did not mind, because, at the end of the day, I knew that, deep down, he loved me and that he would never leave me. The good thing was that whenever he was coming back from his business trips, he would always bring me back a gift. Guilty gifts, Curtis. That behaviour only started after he had started to play outside. Once, after he came back from Sweden, he gave me that really nice Storm watch. Gee, she must have been good, the Swedish girlfriend!

That's all there is to it, really. Should I be blessed again with finding a new companion, I don't want to have just a marriage, but a real relationship that is lived and felt and grows stronger day by day.

So, when I am feeling a little bit strange every time I think of you or when we are chatting, this is very troublesome for me, even more so because we have not even met face to face. You see, that is why I had initially said to you that we should take it as it comes, but I was not expecting to get all fuzzy inside just by chatting with you. So that is where my fears are coming from. I am afraid that we will end up developing that fantastic connection through messenger and, when we meet, realise that we have no connection at all.

I surely don't know how you managed to get to me so quickly, but you did and I was not even looking.

As I am searching for rational answers in this very strange (yet, very pleasurable) experience, I actually read again that first long email you wrote to me. It did put a warm smile on my face. You will have to tell me about all these women you met and why, in your eyes, they were not good wife material. What do you mean by that anyway? If you are looking for someone to cook, clean and iron your shirts... get a cleaning lady... If you are looking for someone to love you just the way you are, support you and comfort you... Well... you may have knocked on the right door as long as, in return, I get the strong, caring, loving man whom I can see in your eyes.

So, if you happen to catch this email before you go to bed, then imagine that I am tenderly massaging your head, your neck, shoulders and the bottom of your back, kissing you softly all the way as I am relieving all the stiffness and tension from your, no doubt, very gorgeous, strong body... Gee, that thought alone is making me want to jump on plane to YABA, and you better avoid dark corners, as you would be in great danger of being ravished by me.... But, of course, I cannot tell you things like that as we have THE PLAN...

Thinking of you as I am now going to bed...

Lorie

PS: do you know that I sleep naked?... May be...

Lorie re-read her note to Curtis. Until that moment, she had just fed him a little bit here and a little bit there about her past, but had not discussed her previous marriage with him, as she thought it was something very private and, although it had not quite turned out be the marriage she would have hoped for, she still appreciated the fact that her relationship with her husband was, on the surface, much better than most of the other married woman she would come across these days. Her and her husband had, over the years, developed a dynamic, seeming to have their own individual space, but they still pursued the same goals. Even after all those years, they did enjoy travelling together and going away for short weekend breaks. By opening up to Curtis, she felt that she was, in a way, exposing herself, but she also believed that, unless they both understood the other's marital past, the good, bad and ugly part, they would probably end up having the wrong expectations of one another should the relationship travel down the matrimonial road.

However, and despite the serious subject matter, she wanted to be sure to keep the note light hearted, and put the PS as yet again another dare to test his reaction.

Satisfied with her write up, she took herself to bed and fell asleep faster than she could even think about it. The deep sleep she had fallen into was short lived as, as if operated by remote control, Lorie opened her eyes, got out of bed, threw her dressing gown over her shoulders and ran downstairs to her office. It spooked her badly to see that her messenger was flashing.

CURTIS WELLS (3/5/2010 10:51:54 PM): *Hello L*
CURTIS WELLS (3/5/2010 10:51:55 PM): *are you there*
CURTIS WELLS (3/5/2010 11:08:32 PM): *<ding>*

Oh, okay, she thought. *A little late for the prom, but he did show up eventually.* Judging by the time Curtis had actually come online, it would have meant midnight her time, as Nigeria was one hour behind her. *This guy must be having a laugh,* she told to herself. What did he expect pinging her at such an unsocial hour? She put her laptop back on snooze and went up to bed.

Lorie could not really find her sleep again, as if she was waiting for something. After tossing and turning for a couple of hours, also, she gave up on the idea of having a lie in, and found herself drawn to her laptop like magnet to metal, and, sure enough, she found this time an email that Curtis had written to her during the night

From: curtiswells62@xxxxxx
To: loriefinnighan@xxxxxx
Subject: Lorie
Date: Saturday, Mar 6, 2010 01:30am

Hello, Lorie,

Thanks for the email. I was so glad to read from you.
I have already enjoyed reading about you and your marriage, and now I know we do have something in common and, well, I will say that everything happens for a reason and I am really looking forward to meeting you. Marriage difficulty is tough, but it is a phase of life that we have to go through, but, you know, reading your story is making me want to meet you soonest even more. I am sorry that I am online and you're not, 'cos I really want to talk to you online. I wish that I did not have to miss you. If only you be with me always, I know I could never be any happier. But again, I know that the day will come when I will be able to spend all my waking moments with you.
I even miss you when I am sleeping! Now I really need that massage, 'cos you make me want it even more.

Hugs and kisses,
Curtis.

She read the message, trying to slowly absorb the words that were in front of her. Although she did not feel indifferent to the warm, loving message, it appeared to her more as something from a *Romeo and Juliet*-type novel rather than real life. Feeling somewhat accelerated by the note, she pressed the 'reply' button.

From: loriefinnighan@xxxxxx
To: curtiswells62@xxxxxx
Subject: Good Morning Babe
Date: Saturday, March 6, 2010. 4:48am

Whoa! You don't hold back much, do you?
As you can see from the ungodly time of my email, I also seem to have sleeping disorders. And yes, I am with you about things happening for a reason.
I really want to chat online with you too, Big Guy.
Missed you a ... lot... last night... NOT GOOD! Who do you think you are to appear in my life like that and made me want to... fall... in... love... all over again. BAD, Curtis! But it feels so good, though.
So tell me, what do two handsome men like you both do on a Saturday? For me, well, I will do my usual. I will go to my gym class (I call it my physical asset management), do the grocery shopping for the week, and clean my car. It is soooo dirty, I cannot stand it anymore. Plus I'll catch up on my house, which looks like it was been hit by hurricane some time between Tuesday and Wednesday, I guess. It would appear that damn cleaning lady is on holiday again... No... wait, I don't have a cleaning... That explains the situation, then... Damn!
I also intend to have a wonderful chat with some guy who is somewhere in Africa; if he happens to show up online, that is...

Later, Gator
Lorie

Totally letting her guard down, Lorie let out on the email the fact that he had been on her mind a lot more than she wanted to accept. As she did not want the email to be dominated by her heart-opening move, she had consciously extended her message by addressing more grounded life subjects, such as asking him asking him about his weekend plans, and sharing hers in the process.

She looked at the clock and toyed with the idea of going back to bed for a couple of hours or giving herself an early start on her weekly disaster-recovery housework, as she called it, before going to her Keep Fit class. As she felt quite energetic, she opted for the early start, and ran upstairs to make her good-morning coffee.

Looking through her kitchen window as the coffee was dripping slowly into the pot, all sorts of questions were crossing her head. For the first time, she started to consider the fact that maybe there was more to this developing online romance than she had initially bargained for. She had initially gone into this Internet dating scheme more out of curiosity than with expectations of actually meeting someone. The previous contacts that she had made had been, for sure, very entertaining, and she had basically found it extremely easy to tell them where to go when she felt that they had overstepped the marks.

Curtis Wells was a different outfit altogether.

She spent the whole morning going through her usual Saturday routines, her mind completely somewhere else, more like in cyberspace than on what she was actually doing.

As she walked back through her front door, her welcome committee was at the rendezvous, going through her shopping bags like a couple of sniffer dogs at the airport, looking for their weekly treat.

After distributing out the goodies to the doggies, Lorie put away her shopping and ran upstairs to get changed and continue her house cleaning, which she had started much earlier that morning. She loaded the washing machine, and went to her laptop to check her emails. She read the new email, not quite sure how to take it, but at least he seemed

to have a sense of humour, which she liked. Another email
from the man himself popped up, informing her that he was
online and asking her to connect.

As she engaged in the conversation, she decided to go
right out at him.

You are not getting any younger, girl, she told herself
and, without wasting time on frivolities, she opened the
exchange with a straight shot:

LORIE.FINNIGHAN(3/7/2010 12:12:45 AM): *you know... I have
   heard from a lot of people that it is always better the 2nd
   time around*
CURTIS WELLS (3/7/2010 12:14:29 AM): *yes me too I want a
   real relationship and then we can decide if we want to tie
   the knot*
LORIE.FINNIGHAN (3/7/2010 12:14:41 AM): *you are funny*

Lorie thought that the man was putting it all in rather
simplistic way. In a time where divorce had rocketed sky
high, and taking into account that the man himself had
already gone through a failed marriage, she could not help
but think that his approach was somewhat very light, naïve,
even. So she decided to grill him a little further.

LORIE.FINNIGHAN(3/7/2010 12:14:56 AM): *please define what
   you mean by a real relationship*
CURTIS WELLS (3/7/2010 12:18:04 AM): *thought you said the
   same thing*

Hein, hein! From his pushed-back answer, it was clear that
he was not ready to venture out further on the topic, so she
gave him an easy escape out of the burning 'r' topic.

LORIE.FINNIGHAN (3/7/2010 12:18:22 AM): *just playing with
   you*
LORIE.FINNIGHAN (3/7/2010 12:18:49 AM): *hey, don't they*

have telephones in Yaba?

CURTIS WELLS (3/7/2010 12:19:42 AM): *they do lol*

CURTIS WELLS (3/7/2010 12:20:00 AM): *I am sure we will get to talk soon okay*

CURTIS WELLS (3/7/2010 12:20:09 AM): *probably next week*

Strange, she thought. *Everyone has a mobile phone these days.*

LORIE.FINNIGHAN(3/7/2010 12:21:09 AM): *don't sweat it, Babe. thing is that if you were to give me a number, I could call you.. It would be strange to hear your voice*

Whilst they were chatting away, Lorie had realised that, although she had seen his picture, she had no idea what he sounded like. Putting a voice to that picture would be quite interesting, she thought, as Curtis' way of keeping everything close to his chest, being secretive, was starting to bother her.

CURTIS WELLS (3/7/2010 12:21:34 AM): *oh yea I like strange occurrences*

LORIE.FINNIGHAN (3/7/2010 12:21:41 AM): *?*

LORIE.FINNIGHAN(3/7/2010 12:23:28 AM): *okay Midnight Man...this girl needs to go to sleep and you should do too... chat tomorrow?*

CURTIS WELLS (3/7/2010 12:23:50 AM): *I wish I could lie in your arms*

Looking at this answer, she got quite taken by surprise. *Sweet, but a little bit too sweet for me right now,* she thought. However, she was not going to discourage him, and decided to reply to him along his lines, with a cherry on top, as they say.

LORIE.FINIGHAN(3/7/2010 12:24:53 AM): *and I wish I could*

*feel your strong arms around me too... tender kisses to
you special man*
LORIE.FINNIGHAN(3/7/2010 12:25:00 AM): *chat tomorrow?*
CURTIS WELLS (3/7/2010 12:25:43 AM): *you too baby*
CURTIS WELLS (3/7/2010 12:25:47 AM): *we will talk tomorrow
okay*

To close her conversation, she sent him the hug emoticon,
paying attention this time not to pick the wrong one, as she
had previously done during one of their earlier messenger
conversations.

LORIE.FINNIGHAN(3/7/2010 12:26:31 AM): *and this is the right
one, for this time*
CURTIS WELLS (3/7/2010 12:26:42 AM): *sure thanks*

Lorie enjoyed her Sunday mornings; she allowed herself to
lie in until 8 a.m., unless Lady had decided otherwise and
attacked her relentlessly until she gave into the pooch and
got up. On Sunday mornings, she took life extremely
slowly and made a point of taking time to prepare herself a
nice breakfast with fresh rolls from the village petrol
station, read through the pile of advertisements that had
multiplied in her letter box over the week, and just let the
morning drift by pottering around.

    She carried on with her housework tasks, threw out the
afternoon and, after walking her two companions whilst
cooking the doggy pasta under the watchful eyes of Lady,
she gave her mother the weekly Sunday call to reassure her
that she had survived the week and there was nothing
special to report on her side.

    She sat with her food tray in her living room, enjoyed
tucking into her grilled chicken, and distracted herself with a
rental DVD, which she had picked up the day before from
the Monti Video rental shop.

After clearing up her kitchen, Lorie went up to the bathroom to clean her face and put on her night moisturiser; not that she thought that it made any difference to her face, but she felt that at least she was doing something nice for herself and enjoyed the refreshing feel of the lotion on her skin. Once her beauty ritual had been completed, she went down to her office and checked her bank balance. *Yuk! Oh well,* she thought, *it will get better... eventually!* At least she felt that it seemed to be going the right way, which somewhat gave her a feel-good factor.

Checking her bank account reminded her of Curtis and that she had offered to help him out.

Where is the devil, anyway, she suddenly thought. Lorie opened a chat window on her messenger.

(3/7/2010 10:12:32 PM): *where are you, lust of mine?*

She nearly fell of her chair to see a response come right back at her:

CURTIS WELLS (3/7/2010 11:03:52 PM): *hey baby*
CURTIS WELLS (3/7/2010 11:04:23 PM): *gimme some minutes trying to tuck Webby Jnr.*
LORIE.FINNIGHAN(3/7/2010 11:27:12 PM): *sure*
LORIE.FINNIGHAN(3/7/2010 11:54:10 PM): *Webby Snr.! I really need to go to bed... but I would love a quick chat with you first. my alarm goes off at 5:30 in the morning, you know!*

Lorie thought it was kind of late for a six-year-old to still be kicking around, but Curtis and his son might have been out late that particular day.

As Curtis was not returning, she checked out as she, on the other hand, had well overstepped her own school night bedtime.

Without really seeing it happening, Curtis had taken a place in Lorie's little private world of which she tended to be very protective. She suffered tremendously from the fact that, in her mind, she was not giving enough attention to her mother and daughter, as, each day, she seemed to be swimming against the current just to protect herself and keep up with work and life demands. So, in her free time, she felt at her happiest when she was by herself with her two dogs, enjoying the peacefulness of her house. She valued, tremendously, Maggie's friendship, and more so that they both seemed to be satisfied to meet up as and when it was convenient for the two of them, and neither of them felt pressurised by the other to re-arrange their own schedules to fit the other. However, it was clear that she had now added a new component to the 'org. chart' of her little world. That component was called Curtis, and Curtis was on her mind a lot more than she would have liked, and she even found that, suddenly, she needed to have a late-night chat with the man.

Who is he, she kept asking herself. He had reluctantly discussed his business venture with her, only because he was caught with his back against the wall when he could not find the cash to get the pump shipped out; he still kept everything close to his chests and was even more secretive about his two business partners. He obviously still had strong connections with Los Angeles, which might explain why he would come online so late in the night, and there was the 'three passport' story. Curtis had revealed to her that he was half Italian and half Irish, but that he held three passports, one of which was a US one. He was definitely turning into quite a fascinating character in her eyes.

5

Perfect Couple Dynamic

To give him an indication of her expectation of him to be online that particular evening, she dropped him a quick email, not forgetting the compulsory little touch of humour, which was her self-defence mechanism whenever she felt exposed emotionally:

From: loriefinnighan@xxxxxx
To: wellscurtis62@xxxxxx
Subject: Will you be on line tonight?
Date: Monday, March 8, 2010, 4:03 PM

Hi, Babe,

It looks as if I will be pulling a late one again tonight; will I have the pleasure of your company on messenger whilst I am working, and you are watching football or something?
Seeing that we already have the perfect couple dynamic?

Lorie

She just closed her short note with her name, cutting out any type of endearing salutation as, although she had opened already during some of their previous communications, she did not want him to think that he had the deal all made and sealed. Furthermore, as much as Curtis seemed to have become a little more than just some Internet guy, she reminded herself regularly that he was just some guy from the Internet with whom she enjoyed playful chats.

From: curtiswell@xxxxxx
To: loriefinnighan @xxxxxx
Subject: Re: Will you be on line tonight?
Date: Mon, March 8. 2010 16:35:55

Hello, Sweetness,

Perfect couple dynamic, huh? That is sweet, anyway... I am so sorry I missed you online; don't be cross with me; I am sure you must have been tired waiting, 'cos you have been running through my mind.
  I miss you so much, darling.
  I believe we will have a lot of time to talk tomorrow.

Love always,
Curtis.

Holy smoke, she thought as she read his email, her eyes fixating on the 'darling' and 'love always' parts of the message. That guy was definitely moving fast; a little too fast, but she could not deny that it did give her a sense of warmth. It has been a long time since she had heard these words spoken to her, let alone written to her. So she allowed herself to dwell for few minutes on the email to savour it, and replied there and then, keeping her message light hearted and teasing to see how he would react.

From :loriefinnighan@xxxxxx
To: wellscurtis62@xxxxxx
Subject: Will you be on line tonight? the sequel
Date: Tuesday, March 9, 2010, 4:54 AM

Hey, Babe,

Aren't we full of ourselves? Waiting for you, Pfff... I was not, too... okay a nerve did get pinched a little, as you did not get back, but, on the other hand, I thought you were jealous of this other guy. He is a serious contender for the top man spot; that's for sure.

Running through your mind, hein? How about running back to Germany? Those arms of mine are desperately missing a strong, sexy babe, like you...

Judging by how the week started, I, for sure, will be online again tonight, so... how about it, Big Guy? Fancy an MSN play date with Lorie?

Tender and eager kisses,
Lorie

PS: I hate you, Webby... 🌀 *How dare you...*

For the following few days, Lorie grew more and more anxious each day, as she was not getting any messages or emails from Curtis. The man seemed to have vanished into thin air. She had picked up on his pattern of login in rather late at night as she would catch in the mornings, emails which he would have obviously written during the night. Despite the fact that he communicated regularly with her, she could not help but find it strange that one minute he would be extremely sharing on his feelings towards her and the next minute he would appear to have disappeared from the face of the Earth without warning. That also reminded her that she had no contact number for him, just an address in Yaba.

The rest of the day just evaded her as, before she knew it, it was close to midnight and, although she was sitting back in her office at home, she did not feel as if she had moved away from her laptop the whole day.

Baberuth was lying under her feet, sleeping extremely deeply, judging by the noises he was making, and Lady had found herself a cushy spot on the sofa across from Lorie's desk, with her two huge, perked-up ears and big round eyes fixated on Lorie.

Checking the time, she felt a little disappointed that Curtis had not shown up online, but, before calling it a night, she left a short message to him on messenger, which he would pick up next time he logged in.

(3/8/2010 12:08:06 AM): *Babe, it is past midnight now... I must get to bed. You probably have fallen asleep yourself with Webby Jnr. I have sent you an email earlier on; have a look at it and tell me what you think... Gee, Big Guy, can't write a to a girl that you miss her badly and 'love always', then keep her hanging until past midnight... That is just not playing nice...*
(3/8/2010 12:08:13 AM): *have a great night, Babe.*

As she was about to close her messenger, a message popped up.

CURTIS WELLS (3/8/2010 12:11:00 AM): *hey baby*

This guy is having a laugh, she thought.

CURTIS WELLS (3/8/2010 12:11:22 AM): *Webby Jnr. is being stubborn but I am sure he will fall asleep soon*
LORIE.FINNIFHAN (3/8/2010 12:12:09 AM): *it is pas midinight !*
CURTIS WELLS (3/8/2010 12:12:16 AM): *but I guess he*

should be asleep by now

LORIE.FINNIGHAN (3/8/2010 12:12:33 AM): *I thought   you had fallen asleep with him*

CURTIS WELLS (3/8/2010 12:12:59 AM): *nope baby*

LORIE.FINNIGHAN(3/8/2010 12:13:11 AM): *did you   see my email*

CURTIS WELLS (3/8/2010 12:13:39 AM):*I haven't checked my emails yet l*

CURTIS WELLS (3/8/2010 12:13:55 AM): *just only logged on my IM so you can see that I am online*

CURTIS WELLS (3/8/2010 12:13:59 AM): *do you have to go to bed now*

LORIE.FINNIGHAN(3/8/2010 12:14:23 AM): *have look a real quick. I will wait for you... I have missed you so much today, you devil!*

CURTIS WELLS (3/8/2010 12:15:59 AM): *hmm now I am eager to see what you wrote*

LORIE.FINNIGHAN (3/8/2010 12:16:13 AM): *read it quick*

CURTIS WELLS (3/8/2010 12:16:34 AM): *okay*

CURTIS WELLS (3/8/2010 12:19:32 AM): *just saw it babe*

CURTIS WELLS (3/8/2010 12:19:44 AM): *thanks so much*

After lots of back and forth on whether Lorie should or should not send Curtis the cash so that the pumps could be shipped out, she could not stop herself from being curious about him, and decided to gamble by sending him the cash, despite her reservations. After work, Lorie had made a detour by the airport and wired the cash to Curtis via Western Union. Once she got home, she scanned the WU ticket, attached it to an email, and sent it to him.

As time was going by, Lorie had found companionship in Curtis. Communicating with him was easy and, to a certain extent, relaxing to her. She did not have to switch on the 'everything is all right' act the way she did with her mother or daughter. With Curtis, she could just let it out, just the way it was at that very moment, and he always seemed to find the right thing to say back to her. The simple fact that she deeply felt those words as she wrote them to him brought her back to her self-protective mode and, as if she had fallen off her horse, she got straight back on it to pursue the conversation.

LORIE.FINNIGHAN(3/8/2010 12:29:28 AM): *and to finish off, when we are finally meeting in the flesh, if you don't like what you see at first glance, you better run Forest... 'cos...you are going to get it real good Boy!*

CURTIS WELLS (3/8/2010 12:30:23 AM): *I want to have it real, Baby!*

LORIE.FINNIGHAN(3/8/2010 12:30:57 AM): *Good! 'Cos I am all system GO... no pumps or Ethanol needed here...just YOU. LOL*

CURTIS WELLS (3/8/2010 12:31:28 AM): *OKAY, Baby*

LORIE.FINNIGHAN3/8/2010 12:31:49 AM): *Have a great night. Wish I could cuddle up against your strong body.*

As she closed the conversation with Curtis, she felt deep tension in her, wondering if she had done right thing by extending him the cash. She recollected then how little she knew of him, but she was growing more and more curious about him. Despite warning alarms bell ringing inside her head, some strange force was driving her to keep up with this mystery man. There was very little else she could do but just wait and see how he would be following through.

6

1 4 3

5:30 a.m. *Here we go again!*

When Lorie opened her eyes, she felt as if she had never gone to bed. That was never a good sign. The day was going to be a long, long one.

As her brain was slowly kicking into the new day, she slowly recollected her late-night conversation with Curtis and went down to her computer to see if he had left her a late-night note and, to her delight, he had.

From: curtiswells62@xxxxxx
To: loriefinnighan@xxxxxx
Ref: Will you be online tonight? the sequel
Date: Tuesday March, 9, 2010 00:12am

Hello, Love,

I am certainly up for it, OKAY. I love competition, you know, and I can really fight for my woman (lol). I hope you had a wonderful night of sleep; I saw that you were still online this AM, but seems that you were idle and not on the computer. I will surely look forward to talk to you tonight about running to Germany to wrap myself around you. I really cannot wait for that to happen. I will, for sure, be happy to know that the pumps are leaving this week.

151

Kisses and hugs,
Curtis

After stopping at the village bakery to pick up her morning breakfast and a coffee to go, she hit the motorway to go to the office. She drove the all forty-five kilometres on complete autopilot, twisting and turning their previous night's conversation in her head. She needed to find a way to regain control of her own mind, as she had been way too consumed by her somewhat strange relationship. With the way things were going in the office, she had kind of worked out that this would not be a long-term story, but, for now, she needed to do her best to make it work, push or shove, until she could find a new job. Going around with her head constantly in the clouds was definitely not the right way to go about it, she kept telling herself; furthermore, she hated herself for the fact that she voluntarily was keeping contact with her mother and Jane as minimal as possible in order not to run the risk of alerting them that she was somewhat unhappy at work and letting out, without intent, that some guy from an Internet dating website was absorbing all her spare moments, as she was trying to figure him out. Despite her earlier made decision to block him out for the day, she just could not resist answering to his email before getting down to her work

Lorie re-read Curtis' note, smiling at the way he had picked up on her playfulness and gone along with it. She started to lose grasp of her emotions and threw back a heartfelt response to him.

From: loriefinnighan @xxxxxx
To: curtswells62@xxxxxx
Subject: Will you be on line tonight? the sequel
Date: Tuesday, March 9, 2010, 8:17 AM

You make me feel so alive, Curtis. I truly thank you for that....

I L.... Y.... NO, I will not say it!

A few weeks had elapsed since Curtis and Lorie had entered into negotiations with each other. These negotiations were not just about making some financial agreement over some ethanol pumps, but also emotional ones.

After Lorie had parted with her cash to Curtis, she suddenly felt as if reality was bringing her feet back on the ground as fast as a loose elevator coming down ten floors without stopping. It horrified her to realise that she had been so preoccupied with dealing with her staffing challenges during the day and negotiating with Curtis during the night, just making time in between to cater for her dogs and keep the house going somehow, that she had barely given any time to her daughter. That night, she made a point of making Jane the first person she would call after work and, God willing, she might even be able to catch her online, as mother and daughter did enjoy bouncing back and forth on messenger with each other from time to time.

That night, she enjoyed reconnecting with her daughter, and also made a point of calling Maggie, to whom she had not spoken to for a while, either. These people were her world and she needed to let them know that.

During one of their short conversations, she told Curtis that she needed to give some attention to her mother and daughter as, between her job and wanting to help him out, she had, in a way, ignored them but, despite that, she was happy to have him around, as he kind of made her feel alive, as he was bringing something completely different into her life, which she enjoyed greatly. The next day, Lorie found yet another email from Curtis, which she did not quite know what to do with.

To: loriefinnighan@xxxxxx
From: curtiswells62@xxxxxx
Subject: No subject.
Date: Tuesday March, 9. 2010 09.21am

No, Lorie, I think the reverse is the case; you make me feel truly alive and you can just say 143; I will still understand what it means. But, all the same, you are welcome.

Curtis

The following morning, as she logged onto her computer, she saw on offline message that Curtis had left earlier that morning.

CURTIS WELLS (3/9/2010 08:53:17): *Hello Baby*
CURTIS WELLS (3/9/2010 08:53:17): *143*

That little unexpected note from Curtis really put her in a great mood for the day. Everything seemed to be going very smoothly for a change, as Lorie went through her day extremely light on her feet, and felt really in control of her environment, which had not happened for way too long. That evening, she made a point of calling Sophie for a catch up. Poor Sophie was still caught in her work dilemma and still negotiating with the Norwegian company, as she was trying to weigh out if she should make the move or not, which, apparently, seemed the be the big show stopper in closing the deal. Lorie listened to her friend attentively and was thanking God that she wasn't in Sophie's position. In Lorie's mind, having to move house and start a brand new life in a foreign country where you do not master the language was all too familiar to her, and she just would not know what to do if she was to be put in that position again. As their conversation went on, the topic slowly moved away from work life to a more complex subject, which was their respective love lives, or there lack of when it came to the two women.

Lorie had told the story of the engineers to Sophie, but, since then, she had not really shared that she had actually set her eyes on a particular one and booted out the others. Lorie gave Sophie a brief summary of the situation with Curtis being in Nigeria and that they were hoping to meet up very soon.

Sophie found the whole story rather catching and told her to keep her up to date as things progressed.

Once they finished their conversation, Lorie checked her computer, but found neither email or messenger notes from Curtis, who was showing offline. As she was tired anyway and it was getting late, she decided to call it a night.

* * *

The following morning, after having battled with the damn alarm clock for thirty minutes, as she just did not feel ready to face the world, her craving for that first cup of coffee got the better of her and, as every morning, she checked her emails whilst enjoying the hot, fresh brew.

She felt very disappointed, and even irritated, to see that there were no late messages from Curtis and, on the spur of the moment, shared her frustrations with him about his online antisocial habits.

From:lorie finnighan@xxxxxx
To: curtiswells62@xxxxxx
Subject:Good Morning
Date:Wednesday, March 10. 2010 05:58am

Good morning, Babe,

Judging by the time, I checked out in the evening for working the graveyard shift, you sure do come online late. I would rather not comment on the kind of days I am having right now. Yesterday, I had some serious heavy metal in the office as the knives came out. It got to the point that the CFO intervened. It is not pretty, but I am hopeful that things will improve very shortly.

So tell me, what on earth is keeping you so occupied each evening? And don't you dare say it is our little Webby Jnr.; that is a poor shot. From what I have read and the great picture I look at every day, he is an adorable child.

Baberuth and Lady are doing great. Joshua will have a lot of fun with little Lady; she is really amazing and wants to play all the time.

I am as excited as I am anxious to meet you, too, Big Guy.

I hope that I will catch you online tonight, but pfff! I am not holding my breath. No need to play tough guy to make yourself desired; you ARE.

Big hug and kisses everywhere,
Lorie

Her day went without surprises, good or bad, and she was happy to make it home at a reasonable time for a change. Taking advantage of the earlier return, she gave the living room a quick go over, went through her post and decided that evening that she would watch one of the DVDs that she had picked from her large home collection, which had built over the years. Getting her mind off Curtis had become a daily struggle for her, and she was haunted day and night by this man and how this story would end up turning out.

As she did not want to miss him should he decide to log in on messenger, she turned her laptop in a way that it would be facing the sofa so that she could keep an eye on it. She went back up to the kitchen, quickly filled a bowl with some cereal, as she could not be asked to prepare dinner, put it on her tray with a pot of tea, and went back down to her office.

With her two pooches on either side of her, she got comfortable, so much so that she ended up falling asleep on the office sofa. By the time she woke up, it was 5 a.m. and the television was still on. It took a few minutes for her to find her marks again. She looked at her laptop, which had gone down through the lack of activity, sprang to her feet and brought it back on. During the night, an email from Curtis had come through.

From: curtiswells62@xxxxxx
To: loriefinnighan@xxxxxx
Subject: Good Night Babe
Date: Wednesday, March 10, 2010 12:09 am

Hello, Baby,

How are you doing? I hope you had a great day; anyway, I am sorry that we didn't get to talk online again today, and you know I think it is even very sweet to be desired.

You know I am already looking forward to us meeting as soon as possible.

I can't wait to meet you and I am sure Joshua is looking forward to that, too; oh, sorry, Webby Jnr.; still trying to get used to the name.

Tell Baberuth and Lady that they will be getting a new friend soon, okay.

Love,
Curtis

During the previous couple of weeks, Curtis and Lorie had approached the subject of them meeting, and it became a topic that they would touch on through all their emails and messenger conversations. The only problem was that Curtis did not seem to have any day set for him and Joshua to travel back to Germany. It was very frustrating to Lorie and, no matter how she tried to understand the issue, Curtis kept secretive and was incredibly good at evading the subject.

That evening, Lorie found a message from Curtis.

From: curtiswells62@xxxxxx
To: loriefinnighan@xxxxxx
Subject: Good Night Babe
Time: Wednesday March 10, 2010 17:26 PM

Hello, Love,

I hope you are not working yourself out in work; well, you know sometimes I may get busy with paper works, and also Webby Jnr. But I will watch the soccer match today and hopefully we will be able to chat later tonight.
I can't wait to meet you, my love...

Love,
Curtis

Finally, a little bit of insight, she thought, but she did not quite understand what kept Curtis so occupied during the day. Even more so since the pump deal was supposedly finished.

She got herself busy pottering around her office, filing some of her papers. Satisfied that the room looked somewhat in order, she decided to switch off her laptop and go to bed. As she was closing her email box, she saw the little box on the right bottom corner of her screen informing her that Curtis had just logged in.

Curtis Wells (3/10/2010 10:57:47pm): *Hello Sweetheart*
Lorie Finnighan (3/10/2010 10:58:18pm): *Who are you?*

Lorie could not believe it. *Does this man ever sleep, or maybe he never wakes up during the day,* she thought.

Curtis Wells (3/10/2010 10:57:47 PM): *Hello sweetheart*
Lorie.Finnighan(3/10/2010 10:58:18 PM): *Who are you?*
Curtis Wells (3/10/2010 11:01:26 PM): *your 4*
Lorie.Finnighan(3/10/2010 11:01:37 PM): *is that so?*
Curtis Wells (3/10/2010 11:01:56 PM): *yes baby*
Lorie.Finnighan(3/10/2010 11:02:02 PM): *good answer!*
Lorie.Finnighan(3/10/2010 11:02:58 PM): *I have missed you, those past few days, you know...you are bad, Webby.*
Curtis.Wells(3/10/2010 11:03:32 PM): *and I don't want to miss you that much, but I do*
Lorie.Finnighan(3/10/2010 11:05:13 PM): *so, tell me, when are we going to have mind-blowing sex on the kitchen table then? Mannnnnnn*
Curtis Wells (3/10/2010 11:07:05 PM): *you know I have been really dreaming about that moment*
Lorie.Finnighan(3/10/2010 11:07:26 PM): *really? how?*
Lorie.Finnighan.(3/10/2010 11:07:57 PM): *give me something I can take to bed with me tonight as I really need to go*
Curtis Wells (3/10/2010 11:08:24 PM): *you know we had ice and I was rubbing it on your belly*
(3/10/2010 11:08:35 PM): *now you are talking*
Curtis Wells (3/10/2010 11:08:40 PM): *and then used my hand to push away dishes and some even broke*
Lorie.Finnghan(3/10/2010 11:08:59 PM): *my god!*
Lorie.Finnighan(3/10/2010 11:09:05 PM): *you are weaked*

LORIE.FINNIGHAN(3/10/2010 11:09:09 PM): *but keep going*

CURTIS WELLS (3/10/2010 11:09:24 PM): *placed you on the counter and it was all so very breathtaking passionate love*

LORIE.FINNIGHN(3/10/2010 11:09:47 PM): *man! You are killing me Webby... WHEN ARE YOU BACK?*

CURTIS WELLS (3/10/2010 11:10:34 PM): *well I told you this month certainly... things are working out fine and I must tell you, you are always on my mind and I guess that keeps me going*

LORIE.FINNIGHAN(3/10/2010 11:11:09 PM): *Curtis, you keep saying this month, this month, I thought it was the 18th?*

CURTIS WELLS (3/10/2010 11:11:50 PM): *yes I will have to choose the date and put it on the return ticket*

CURTIS WELLS (3/10/2010 11:11:56 PM): *so brace yourself*

CURTIS WELLS (3/10/2010 11:12:06 PM): *sound like I am in for some wild sex here*

LORIE.FINNIGHAN(3/10/2010 11:12:21 PM): *you bet!*

CURTIS WELLS (3/10/2010 11:12:50 PM): *hmm*

(3/10/2010 11:12:53 PM): *but, only fuelled with all those love feelings that seem to have taken over me...*

(3/10/2010 11:13:24 PM): *I wish I could tell you what you are doing to me right now...*

CURTIS WELLS (3/10/2010 11:13:37 PM): *tell me*

(3/10/2010 11:14:47 PM): *you have set to light my whole body and you know what that means/*

(3/10/2010 11:17:15 PM): *that if I can not have you between my legs, than I will be having that wonderful, sweet...orgasm all by myself wishing we could share this together*

(3/10/2010 11:19:16 PM): *all those emotions you have brought back to life are making me want you, again and again and again....how far is the airport/*

(3/10/2010 11:20:08 PM): *what are you doing Curtis?--need any help?*

CURTIS WELLS (3/10/2010 11:20:46 PM): *are you excited already baby*

CURTIS WELLS (3/10/2010 11:21:10 PM): *please don't have*

the orgasm alone yet baby, I want us to have it together

(3/10/2010 11:23:07 PM): *Holly Moley Curtis... damn, I wish I could kiss you, your beautiful neck, go down gently, your belly, the outside of legs,*

(3/10/2010 11:23:22 PM): *gently going to the inside*

(3/10/2010 11:23:26 PM): *up and up*

(3/10/2010 11:23:49 PM): *rub my tongue around you*

CURTIS WELLS (3/10/2010 11:24:04 PM): *rub your tongue around me?*

(3/10/2010 11:24:57 PM): *yes!*

(3/10/2010 11:25:37 PM): *because I want to feel you inside me as I want you so close so close to me and every part of me*

Lorie had by no means anticipated that their conversation would go down the road of messenger sex. Well, she thought, if she could not get the real thing, there was no harm in going for an alternative and, hopefully, it might give the man something to think about in order to speed him up a little.

7

Mrs Webby

Still under the spell of their previous night's indecent conversation, Lorie took a few minutes in the late morning to check her email.

From: wellscurtis62@xxxxxx
To: loriefinnighan@xxxxxx
Subject:
Date: Thursday, March 11. 10:46:14 am

Hi, Love,

Thanks so much for last night's chat; I really enjoyed it... I guess you must be already tired by now, 'cos you have been running through my mind non-stop. You are very sweet and I am so glad to have you, Lorie; you are everything that I ever prayed for and I don't know what life will be like without you.

143 Mrs. Webby :)

Curtis' email went straight through her as she nearly fell of her chair for him calling her Mrs. Webby.

After collecting her thoughts back together and snapping out of the daze she had gone into, she replied to Curtis.

From: loriefinnighan@xxxxxx
To: curtiswells62@xxxxxx
Subject: No subject
Date: Thursday, March 11, 2010 11:00:35 am

A next day emailer, hein! Definitely a keeper. Is this a marriage proposal, Mr. Webby?

To her astonishment, she saw an email coming straight back.

From: curtiswells62@xxxxxx
To: loriefinnighan@xxxxxx
Subject: No subject
Date: Thursday, March 11, 2010.11:19 am

I got to leave the computer now, baby. But, about the proposal, I will do that in person, okay.
Love

"Holy shit!" she screamed in the office.

Lorie had asked Curtis if he was proposing to her as a joke. She was by no means expecting his response, let alone a response at all. *Well*, she thought, *if you are going to scratch the match, girl, you are bound to get burnt!*

This was getting extremely dangerous in her mind, as she needed to keep her feet seriously on the ground and keep in complete touch with her hard realities, which were the job, her daughter, her mortgage, all those things that make one's day-to-day life.

Push back, she thought. *Need to push back immediately.*

From: loriefinnighan@xxxxxx
To: curtiswells@xxxxxx
Subject: no subject
Date: Thursday, March 11, 2010. 11:46:34

*Just pulling your leg, Big Guy... don't sweat it... Make sure to
check back in later, though...*

143

Completely disorientated, Lorie grabbed her mobile and
sent a text message to Maggie, informing her that she had
just received a marriage proposal on email.

It did not take long for Maggie to call her back. Maggie
was the ultimate wisdom in Lorie's eyes, and often played
Devil's advocate when Lorie was faced with a dilemma. For
Maggie, love and magic seemed only to exist in the movies,
as the real world was not that kind. Maggie's voice was the
voice of total shock and horror as she very directly told
Lorie to watch out. This was by far the tensest
conversation Lorie ever recalled having with her friend, and
she promised Maggie that she would be very careful.
Maggie was not convinced at all, as she was obviously
sensing that Lorie was a lot more into the engineer than she
was letting on.

As soon as Lorie got home, she rang Maggie back, as
she was not happy about the way their conversation had
ended earlier that day, and she told her that she appreciated
that her friend was, in a way, being protective towards her
and that was why Maggie's friendship was so valuable to
her, as she needed to have Maggie's voice of reason to bring
her feet back to the ground as much as she needed Sophie,
the optimistic, who would spend hours on the phone
discussing the incredible love story with her and fantasising
how it would turn out. In short, as Sophie was the Romeo

and Juliet type, Maggie was more the 'love and marriage are overrated' type. Lorie needed both to keep her balance to deal with the situation at hand.

8

My Heart

From: curtiswells62@xxxxxx
To: loriefinnighan@xxxxxx
Subject: My Heart
Date: Friday March, 13, 2010. 08:35am

Dear Love,

The first time we were introduced over the computer, Lorie, I knew you were the one for me. The first hello and the first goodbye, we both knew. It has been a little over some days, and we are still fondly in each other's minds, souls and hearts. Before I met you, I had no idea what love really was until my heart truly started aching for you. Every minute we did not chat, and each time I think we are far apart, tears run down my face unconditionally for the longing of you near me, Sweetie. I never knew a woman could have stolen my heart and made it truly hers. I never knew I could love a woman more then my own life. I long for the day I can finally look into your beautiful, soft, kind eyes and tell you how much I love you, baby, and need you. The true beginning of my life is when we will be in our house, and all my dreams are finally coming true. I don't know about all of yours. Seeing you every day is going to be the biggest blessing to my heart, knowing you are in touching reach of me, which does scare me; however, in a wonderful way, my love. You are my every

166

heartbeat, my every gasping breath of life. What I need to survive and make it through this lonely world can only be conquered with you by my side. I do not think there are any words that could describe the way I actually feel about you. All I know is you, dear Lorie, My Love, you are the only woman who is in my mind and heart, the only woman who is in my soul, the only woman who truly and unconditionally has my heart for my lifetime and the many more lifetimes the world has to offer us. When I think about you, my eyes start to water, because I know you are somewhere else and not in my arms. But the thought of you keeps me going and going for another breath of fresh air to keep my longing for you in my life going. I will never leave, and I will truly never hurt you. I admire you. You are my inspiration for anything, and everything, on this cold, damp Earth. I never thought my time would come to love, and then it came and I was hit with so much emotion and power I did not know where to put it all. I have stacked it piece by piece in my heart for you. I truly believe you are my soul mate, and you are the only woman I will give all I have to offer forever. I hope you never let go of me, because I want to love you everlasting, and I know you love me, too, as much as I love you. Just the thought of you brightens my day completely, and sometimes I do bring you there on purpose to make myself happy when I am down. Picturing your smile makes me smile, and I cannot wait to actually see that adoring woman I know with the unforgettable smile I know so soon. I treasure you locked in the big steel safe of my heart. I love you, Lorie, sweetheart, and that is the only thing that is never going to change in my life. Always and truly yours forever.

Hugs and kisses,
Curtis.

"*Oh no! No! No!* That is so not happening," she screamed. *What is this guy trying to do to me now? What's wrong with him? Who writes love emails like this, anyway? Curtis*

Wells, you are pushing it too far this time, she thought, but despite her best efforts to shake out the goose bumps all over her body, she just could not fight the feelings she was experiencing at that moment. She had fallen hard for the guy and she could no longer deny it to herself. Who was he? After all this time, she was no nearer to an answer to the answer, yet she truly was in love with this stranger.

After Curtis had dropped the bomb email on her, she did not get to hear from him for over twenty-four hours. She just did not understand and her confusion levels were sky high.

She spent her entire Saturday just hovering, hoping that Curtis would contact her. The whole day went by. As she could not find sleep, she went down to her office and sent an email to Curtis instead.

To: curtiswell62@xxxxxx
From: loriefinnighan@xxxxxx
Subject: My Heart
Date: Saturday, March 13, 2010: 12:01 am

I don't understand, Curtis. I could not wait today to chat with you, and now it is midnight and I am going to bed, Curtis.
   What is monopolising you so much?
   You will be in my dreams, Curtis, but please, if all those beautiful and wonderful words are truly felt by you, then I am sure that you will find some time for us tomorrow.

Hugs and kisses,
Lorie

The next morning, to her relief, Lorie woke up to an email from Curtis.

From: curtiswells62@xxxxxx
To: loriefinnighan@xxxxxx
Subject: RE: My Heart is yours
Date: Saturday, 13 Mar.2010 00:50:34

Love, Lorie,

I will sure find time for you, sweetness... I really miss you, and thanks for being there for me. Thoughts of you really get me going and I must say that I am really thanking God, 'cos I have actually found my real missing rib.
I love you and can't wait to be with you.

Curtis

PS: Sorry about the pain, baby...

Lorie went into a rage after reading the note from Curtis, which, in her eyes, did not cut it whatsoever. How could someone write such an emotionally loaded love declaration on one hand and follow it through with a message that more or less person said 'later, Love, I am busy'? Charged with anger, Lorie thought it best to give herself some time before she answered him. Completely frustrated by the note, she ran into the shower, as she wanted to make sure she would make it to her fit class that morning. The exercise would help her to calm down and, if she was lucky enough, take her mind off the email for a while.

By the time she got back home loaded with her shopping bags and the weekly treats for Baberuth and Lady, she was still very uptight, despite her power workout, and decided to fight back and offload by replying to him in her own twisted style.

From: loriefinnighan@xxxxxx
To: wellscurtis62@xxxxxx
Subject: My Heart is your
Date: Saturday, March 13, 2010, 1:02 PM

*Sorry about the pain? News flash, Big Guy! You have,
willingly or not, set that girl's pants on fire, so unless I get just
a little bit of you on messenger, I will have no other option
than calling the fire brigade and jumping the hunky fireman
to calm down a little bit, as D.I.Y. does not seem to cut it any
longer... It will by no means cure me from you... that seems
to be impossible right now, but gee, life can be so unfair
sometimes.*

*Holy smoke! Love hurts... No wonder I kept away from
that L. thing all these years...*

*But despite all the resisting I have been doing, it is clear
to me now that my life will never be the same again, because
of, or, should I say, thanks to, you, Webby, and Webby Jnr.*

I am craving for you, Babe; you better believe it!

Lorie.

Lorie threw the words out like she was throwing knives at a
target. She just would not spare him the emotions. How
could he possibly be so casual about it? She never asked
him to write things like that to her; quite the contrary, she
wanted to stick to the plan of keeping their online
relationship friendly. That 'I am pouring my heart to you'
email was not friendly; in her views, that was a total hostile
takeover of her most precious asset, known to her as her
emotional independence.

Well, obviously her email did not remain unnoticed, as
he had replied to her early that very evening:

From: curtiswells62@xxxxxx
To: loriefinnighan @xxxxxxx
Date: Saturday, Mar 13, 2010. 06:19:21 –0800
Subject: RE: My Heart is yours

Hello, my Love,

I am so glad to know the kind of feeling you are having and, really, I feel so great hearing that I can make a woman feel that way... You know, at some point, I thought that I will never have a feel of what love is like, but I am glad that I have a woman who I can call my own now. Webby Jnr. has been feeling feverish and I even saw you online, but you didn't reply. I will try to check you back online, okay.

Love always,
Your hubby,
Curtis.

Say what! I am married now! Is this man trying to put me in a mental institution?

Lorie could not handle what she viewed as sheer bravado from Curtis. She just did not know what to do with herself as she tried to gasp for air. The 'your hubby' part was proving to be way too much for her to take, on top of the love note.

Okay then, she thought, *if you wish to play happy families ahead of time, then I can do that, too.*

From: lorie finnighan@xxxxxx
To: wellscurtis62@xxxxxx
Subject: My Heart is yours
Date: Saturday, March 13, 2010. 2:53pm

You know best what to do with Webby Jnr., but knowing you guys are in Africa, that makes me a little bit nervous... Don't dwell on taking him to a doctor if you have not done so yet... but, by the look of things, it is my son to be we are talking about here, so don't cut corners, OKAY! I will keep checking to see if you are online every fifteen minutes; otherwise, give me a set time so that I don't miss you again, because... I am MISSING you!

Yours unconditionally,
Lorie

Later on that evening, Lorie finally caught up with Curtis online.

CURTIS WELLS (3/13/2010 10:02:41 PM): *Hello Love*
LORIE.FINNIGHAN(3/13/2010 10:03:41 PM): *HI*
CURTIS WELLS (3/13/2010 10:03:53 PM): *how are you doing baby*
LORIE.FINNIGHAN(3/13/2010 10:04:27 PM): *missing you, what kind of question is that?*
LORIE.FINNIGHAN(3/13/2010 10:04:33 PM): *How is Joshua?*
CURTIS WELLS (3/13/2010 10:05:03 PM): *he is feeling feverish but I am sure he will be fine, at least much better*
LORIE.FINNIGHAN(3/13/2010 10:05:37 PM): *careful here, as I had put in my email to you... you guys are in a funny country*
LORIE.FINNIGHAN(3/13/2010 10:05:51 PM): *he might have caught a bug or something*
CURTIS WELLS (3/13/2010 10:07:57 PM): *well probably we will get a test by Monday to find out*
CURTIS WELLS (3/13/2010 10:08:03 PM): *I really miss you baby, wish you were here*
LORIE.FINNIGHAN(3/13/2010 10:08:12 PM): *Me too, Curtis...*
LORIE.FINNIGHAN(3/13/2010 10:08:33 PM): *That was a really touching email you wrote to me, Babe*
CURTIS WELLS (3/13/2010 10:09:14 PM): *really, well you know it was until after I wrote it that I started wondering everything I wrote*
LORIE.FINNIGHAN(3/13/2010 10:09:27 PM): *what do you mean?*
CURTIS WELLS (3/13/2010 10:10:10 PM): *I was almost in tears*

'cos I found that love actually hurts

LORIE.FINNIGHAN(3/13/2010 10:10:32 PM): *Good!!! at least it is not just me*

CURTIS WELLS (3/13/2010 10:10:58 PM): *yes it is a two way thing*

LORIE.FINNIGHAN(3/13/2010 10:11:02 PM): *but it feels strange and scary what is going on*

LORIE.FINNIGHAN(3/13/2010 10:11:46 PM): *it is like it is the most natural thing in the world*

LORIE.FINNIGHAN(3/13/2010 10:12:07 PM): *as if we have been together for ages or something*

CURTIS WELLS (3/13/2010 10:12:25 PM): *yes I feel the same way too and I am happy that I feel this way*

LORIE.FINNIGHAN(3/13/2010 10:13:12 PM): *Me too Curtis, but right now, I wish I could feel you some other ways...the physical kind of way...*

LORIE.FINNIGHAN(3/13/2010 10:13:34 PM): *or should I call that hunky fireman?*

CURTIS WELLS (3/13/2010 10:14:40 PM): *nope I was about to ask if you already did*

LORIE.FINNIGHAN(3/13/2010 10:14:53 PM): *NO>>>> cos*

LORIE.FINNIGHAN(3/13/2010 10:15:06 PM): *You are the one that I want, Sunshine!*

CURTIS WELLS (3/13/2010 10:16:07 PM): *yes sure I will be the fire man to actually take the pants out and then instead of stopping the fire, I will had more coal so we will be even more heated*

LORIE.FINNIGHAN(3/13/2010 10:17:06 PM): *Oh Sweetheart, forget heated, this is a blaze!!! Can I ask you a question?*

LORIE.FINNIGHANCURTIS WELLS (3/13/2010 10:17:21 PM): *sure*

LORIE.FINNIGHAN(3/13/2010 10:17:53 PM): *Why are you still in Nigeria?*

CURTIS WELLS (3/13/2010 10:18:22 PM): *because soon I will be with you, I am sure it is worth the wait*

CURTIS WELLS (3/13/2010 10:18:34 PM): *the wait will make it even more passionate right*

LORIE.FINNIGHAN(3/13/2010 10:18:48 PM): *you are a funny guy, aren't you?*

CURTIS WELLS (3/13/2010 10:19:17 PM): *don't you like that in me*

LORIE.FINNIGHAN(3/13/2010 10:19:29 PM): *I love that in you,*

LORIE.FINNIGHAN(3/13/2010 10:20:01 PM): *but truly, I think there is enough passion going between us to keep us going for a while, don't you?... No need to wait Curtis, really...*

CURTIS WELLS (3/13/2010 10:20:16 PM): *yes I think so too*

CURTIS WELLS (3/13/2010 10:20:19 PM): *I love you too baby*

LORIE.FINNIGHAN(3/13/2010 10:21:04 PM): *Me too Curtis, no*

LORIE.FINNIGHAN(3/13/2010 10:21:17 PM): *I am in LOVE with you*

LORIE.FINNIGHAN(3/13/2010 10:21:47 PM): *What are you doing Curtis/*

CURTIS WELLS (3/13/2010 10:23:21 PM): *well just watching a dance show on TV and talking to you... then will go to sleep dreaming about you and also checking on our son*

CURTIS WELLS (3/13/2010 10:23:30 PM): *how is my daughter baby*

LORIE.FINNIGHAN(3/13/2010 10:23:46 PM): *She is great! Curtis, you are making me laugh*

LORIE.FINNIGHAN(3/13/2010 10:23:57 PM): *You know*

LORIE.FINNIGHAN(3/13/2010 10:24:55 PM): *I was in the kitchen this evening and thinking about you but it was as if you were coming back home, like we already live together or something... this is not healthy, Curtis*

CURTIS WELLS (3/13/2010 10:25:28 PM): *well then what is healthiness*

LORIE.FINNIGHAN(3/13/2010 10:25:48 PM): *don't know*

CURTIS WELLS (3/13/2010 10:26:22 PM): *well for me I think loving you is what keeps me healthy*

CURTIS WELLS (3/13/2010 10:26:42 PM): *and I think I need to prescribe the same medicine for Joshua but you know he is still a kid*

LORIE.FINNIGHAN(3/13/2010 10:27:30 PM): *yes he is and he is your son, which makes him very special to me*

LORIE.FINNIGHAN(3/13/2010 10:28:09 PM): *I wish I could be with you, Curtis*

CURTIS WELLS (3/13/2010 10:28:24 PM): *me too*

LORIE.FINNIGHAN(3/13/2010 10:29:06 PM): *How are thing going work wise on your side?*

CURTIS WELLS (3/13/2010 10:31:55 PM): *well they are going great, everything with the pumps are fine now... Just that I will have to also secure some documents and I have some financial meetings that kind of bothers me, but I will know what is going on by Monday anyway*

LORIE.FINNIGHAN(3/13/2010 10:32:33 PM): *so does that mean that you are getting close to coming back*

CURTIS WELLS (3/13/2010 10:32:43 PM): *yes baby*

LORIE.FINNIGHAN(3/13/2010 10:32:54 PM): *I will not believe it, you know*

CURTIS WELLS (3/13/2010 10:33:29 PM): *what is that*

LORIE.FINIGHAN(3/13/2010 10:33:49 PM): *I so want to touch you just to confirm to myself that you are real*

CURTIS WELLS (3/13/2010 10:34:24 PM): *well you will do that for sure, and that is the most important thing in my life right now*

CURTIS WELLS (3/13/2010 10:34:34 PM): *spending the rest of my life with you*

LORIE.FINNIGHAN(3/13/2010 10:35:52 PM): *Curtis, things have gone so fast between us, and I would want nothing more than spending of my life falling in love with you as well*

CURTIS WELLS (3/13/2010 10:36:20 PM): *yes I know baby and I want you to know that this is meant to be and it will for sure*

LORIE.FINNIGHAN (3/13/2010 10:36:59 PM): *I want this for us too, Curtis. I guess you are right about us being soul mates*

LORIE.FINNIGHAN(3/13/2010 10:37:22 PM): *I feel so close to you, emotionally in a strange kind of way*

CURTIS WELLS (3/13/2010 10:37:44 PM): *do you think Jany will accept me*

LORIE.FINNIGHAN(3/13/2010 10:38:41 PM): *She will adore you but watch out, if you do not treat me right, she will kick you between the legs so hard you won't walk for months*

CURTIS WELLS (3/13/2010 10:39:11 PM): *well that will not happen for sure*

LORIE.FINNIGHAN(3/13/2010 10:39:12 PM): *btw, she does not like to be called Jany*

(3/13/2010 10:40:04 PM): *Hey, so tell me about our house, the one you referred to in your email? What does it look like?*

CURTIS WELLS (3/13/2010 10:40:49 PM): *a single family home that is my dream*

CURTIS WELLS (3/13/2010 10:40:51 PM): *family*

LORIE.FINNIGHAN(3/13/2010 10:41:35 PM): *We are ambitious, aren't we?*

CURTIS WELLS (3/13/2010 10:42:03 PM): *YEP*

LORIE.FINNIGHAN(3/13/2010 10:42:17 PM): *Curtis, it does not matter what it is like, it is what we make it, which is important*

CURTIS WELLS (3/13/2010 10:42:37 PM): *yes you are right and it will be OUR HOME*

LORIE.FINNIGHAN(3/13/2010 10:42:44 PM): *All right!*

LORIE.FINNIGHAN(3/13/2010 10:42:52 PM): *I better tell you something though*

CURTIS WELLS (3/13/2010 10:43:05 PM): *what...*

(3/13/2010 10:43:34 PM): *Before I can say YES to you, my friend Maggie wants to check you out*

LORIE.FINNIGHAN(3/13/2010 10:43:40 PM): *to see if you are good enough for me*

LORIE.FINNIGHAN(3/13/2010 10:44:03 PM): *you see, I am protected*

CURTIS WELLS (3/13/2010 10:44:33 PM): *who is Maggie*

LORIE.FINNIGHAN(3/13/2010 10:45:02 PM): *Maggie used to be my assistant in my first company and we have kept in touch ever since*

LORIE.FINNIGHAN(3/13/2010 10:45:17 PM): *she is the only friend I get to spend time with here really*

LORIE.FINNIGHAN(3/13/2010 10:46:00 PM): *so although I am no longer her boss, she still protects me the way she did when she was working for me*

LORIE.FINNIGHAN(3/13/2010 10:46:33 PM): *so what else do you have planned for us?*

CURTIS WELLS (3/13/2010 10:47:41 PM): *well I am sure we do have a lot to talk about when we are together baby*

CURTIS WELLS (3/13/2010 10:47:52 PM): *I will sure love to meet her and hope then that I pass her test*

LORIE.FINNIGHAN(3/13/2010 10:48:14 PM): *are you anxious of that day/*

LORIE.FINNIGHAN(3/13/2010 10:49:34 PM): *Curtis, stop watching* the dancing girls and answer me

LORIE.FINNIGHAN(3/13/2010 10:49:42 PM): *this is a very sensitive question*

CURTIS WELLS (3/13/2010 10:51:36 PM): *anxious or nervous*

CURTIS WELLS (3/13/2010 10:51:44 PM): *I think nervous but I will be fine for sure baby*

LORIE.FINNIGHAN(3/13/2010 10:53:05 PM): *where do you think that will be?*

CURTIS WELLS (3/13/2010 10:56:00 PM): *I know when I have you wrapped around me, all the nerves will be fine*

LORIE.FINNIGHAN(3/13/2010 10:56:21 PM): *Me too, Babe*

LORIE.FINNIGHAN(3/13/2010 10:56:57 PM): *one part of me would like to meet you at the airport but another part of me is telling me NO*

CURTIS WELLS (3/13/2010 10:57:30 PM): *well what are we going to do about your other part*

LORIE.FINNIGHAN(3/13/2010 10:58:11 PM): *don't know...thing is I cannot imagine myself being able to sleep that night knowing you are only few kms away from me*

LORIE.FINNIGHAN(3/13/2010 10:58:19 PM): *this is awful, Curtis*

LORIE.FINNIGHAN(3/13/2010 10:58:40 PM): *what do you think?*

CURTIS WELLS (3/13/2010 10:59:37 PM): *well that is what happens when cupid calls*

LORIE.FINNIGHAN(3/13/2010 11:00:10 PM): *that guy again... wait that I catch him*

LORIE.FINNIGHAN(3/13/2010 11:00:38 PM): *are you really my salvation and destiny, Curtis Wells*

CURTIS WELLS (3/13/2010 11:02:16 PM): *brb*

CURTIS WELLS (3/13/2010 11:07:10 PM): *well I think you are my salvation*

LORIE.FINNIGHAN(3/13/2010 11:07:19 PM): *why?*

CURTIS WELLS (3/13/2010 11:08:21 PM): *or I will just say we found each other*

LORIE.FINNIGHAN(3/13/2010 11:08:41 PM): *we sure did, Babe*

LORIE.FINNIGHAN(3/13/2010 11:09:31 PM): *you have no idea how much you touched my heart when you first referred me as Mrs. Webby and talk about Joshua as if he was our son*

CURTIS WELLS (3/13/2010 11:11:36 PM): *oh right, I never knew;*

want to tell me

LORIE.FINNIGHAN(3/13/2010 11:13:00 PM): *hard to explain... I guess it kind of hit me then that you were already a part of my life.*

LORIE.FINNIGHAN(3/13/2010 11:13:55 PM): *but Curtis, do you see us as a family?*

CURTIS WELLS (3/13/2010 11:15:00 PM): *YES*

LORIE.FINNIGHAN(3/13/2010 11:15:27 PM): *What are your dreams of how it should be?*

CURTIS WELLS (3/13/2010 11:16:57 PM): *a loving and peaceful home, where every day seems like it is a new day*

LORIE.FINNIGHAN(3/13/2010 11:17:14 PM): *those are my words, Curtis*

CURTIS WELLS(3/13/2010 11:18:17 PM): *I want to have a warm, loving home for the children and as far as us is concerned, I want my marriage to be an ongoing love affair growing deeper and stronger each day*

CURTIS WELLS (3/13/2010 11:18:18 PM): *I will love my wife unconditionally, and be a good father to my young ones*

CURTIS WELLS (3/13/2010 11:18:38 PM): *yes baby*

CURTIS WELLS (3/13/2010 11:18:49 PM): *will you be my shoulder when I am grey and older*

LORIE.FINNIGHAN(3/13/2010 11:19:19 PM): *Curtis, when we are grey and old, that is where we will have the best times together*

LORIE.FINNIGHAN(3/13/2010 11:20:02 PM): *but Hold on Soldier...I don't want to have another child, I am too old Curtis*

CURTIS WELLS(3/13/2010 11:20:27 PM): *I already have 2 perfect kids, a daughter and a son called Joshua*

CURTIS WELLS (3/13/2010 11:20:54 PM): *I am okay with my two kids Lorie.*

CURTIS WELLS (3/13/2010 11:21:02 PM): *and I want to be able to cater for them*

LORIE.FINNIGHAN(3/13/2010 11:22:18 PM): *You are a strong man, Curtis and just the man I need...I need someone to find comfort in*

CURTIS WELLS(3/13/2010 11:22:34 PM): *and you will always*

have my open arms to come home to

CURTIS WELLS (3/13/2010 11:23:17 PM): *well I already told you, you are my missing rib honey*

LORIE.FINNIGHAN(3/13/2010 11:23:31 PM): *that is so sweet, Webby*

LORIE.FINNIGHAN(3/13/2010 11:24:06 PM): *will you need to travel a lot for your business*

LORIE.FINNIGHAN(3/13/2010 11:26:13 PM): *Curtis, I don't mind... I will always be behind you no matter what, you can bet on that*

LORIE.FINNIGHAN(3/13/2010 11:26:24 PM): *'cos, that is what good wives do, right? ...LOL*

CURTIS WELLS (3/13/2010 11:27:36 PM): *yes baby and I cant wait to be with my baby*

CURTIS WELLS (3/13/2010 11:28:18 PM): *as it is, I may not travel too much business*

LORIE.FINNIGHAN(3/13/2010 11:28:39 PM): *that is good then... how do you know?*

CURTIS WELLS (3/13/2010 11:29:35 PM): *I know because it is my business and I decide that for myself*

LORIE.FINNIGHAN(3/13/2010 11:29:48 PM): *Yes Boss*

LORIE.FINNIGHANS(3/13/2010 11:29:58 PM): *gee, we are masterful are we not?*

CURTIS WELLS (3/13/2010 11:30:13 PM): *nope you are the boss, have you forgotten the woman heads the house*

CURTIS WELLS (3/13/2010 11:30:23 PM): *sorry the man leads and the woman takes care of the house*

LORIE.FINNIGHAN(3/13/2010 11:30:40 PM): *oh, so will I be a housewife then?*

LORIE.FINNIGHAN(3/13/2010 11:30:58 PM): *right now... that sounds delightful trust me*

CURTIS WELLS (3/13/2010 11:31:30 PM): *well you will be busy okay honey*

LORIE.FINNIGHAN(3/13/2010 11:31:50 PM): *I like busy... with what, Honey?*

CURTIS WELLS (3/13/2010 11:31:57 PM): *ME*

LORIE.FINNIGHAN(3/13/2010 11:32:01 PM): *YEAHHHH*

CURTIS WELLS(3/13/2010 11:32:11 PM): *there is a god after all!*

CURTIS WELLS (3/13/2010 11:32:24 PM): *not a small g baby*
CURTIS WELLS (3/13/2010 11:32:26 PM): *God*
LORIE.FINNIGHAN(3/13/2010 11:32:52 PM): *Yep, you are correct...*
(3/13/2010 11:40:33 PM): *Okay, I need to go to bed now... don't want to but I have a lot of catching up to do in my house, so can we chat tomorrow?*
CURTIS WELLS (3/13/2010 11:43:10 PM): *okay honey*
CURTIS WELLS (3/13/2010 11:43:13 PM): *I love you so much*
(3/13/2010 11:44:21 PM): *Me too Webby...*
LORIE.FINNIGHAN(3/13/2010 11:44:45 PM): *You have a great night and please keep an eye on our Little Jnr...*
CURTIS WELLS(3/13/2010 11:45:12 PM): *I will baby, I am sure he will be better*
CURTIES WELLS(3/13/2010 11:45:36 PM): *You will be in my dreams and I will be cuddling up to your warm, secure body and feel like the happiest woman ever*

As she ended the conversation with Curtis, this time, for sure, the horses had been let out of the barn. Lorie struggled a lot with Curtis talking to her about his son, as if he was theirs, referring to her daughter, Jane, as if she was his, discussing their future home as if it was the most natural thing in the world. It appeared to her that he had made an overnight decision that she was his wife and they were already a family, just like that, without a judge and jury or a priest, even. *What now,* she asked herself. Whilst they were chatting, Curtis had also replied to her email telling her that, should Joshua not feel any better, he would be taking him to the hospital for tests, which, in her mind, was the wise thing to do.

For the following few days, Lorie did not really hear from Curtis as Joshua had been kept in hospital following the tests. Through the examinations, it transpired that Joshua had been bitten by some sort of local insect, to which he reacted very badly.

To her relief, she found Curtis back online, which she

saw as a good sign.

CURTIS WELLS(3/17/2010 10:03:24 PM): *hi*

LORIE.FINNIGHAN(3/17/2010 10:06:12 PM): *Curtis, Sweety, you there?*

CURTIS WELLS (3/17/2010 10:09:44 PM): *I am here*

LORIE.FINNIGHAN(3/17/2010 10:10:00 PM): *you don't half give me frights, you know*

CURTIS WELLS (3/17/2010 10:10:20 PM): *sorry baby*

LORIE.WELLS(3/17/2010 10:10:41 PM): *no worries... I thought that I had done or said something wrong*

CURTIS WELLS (3/17/2010 10:11:42 PM): *nope baby you didn't do anything wrong*

CURTIS WELLS (3/17/2010 10:11:50 PM): *I missed you so much honey*

CURTIS WELLS (3/17/2010 10:13:32 PM): *yes I felt it too*

LORIE.FINNIGHAN(3/17/2010 10:13:34 PM): *me too... you have no idea... the hours feel like days when I don't hear from you and it is even worse with Joshua in hospital. How is the little guy* .

CURTIS WELLS (3/17/2010 10:13:36 PM): *he is much better*

LORIE.FINNIGHAN(3/17/2010 10:13:50 PM): *that is a relief...*

LORIE.FINNIGHAN(3/17/2010 10:14:03 PM): *how are things ticking with your business*

CURTIS WELLS (3/17/2010 10:15:30 PM): *well you know I already told you about the 5k, that is what is remaining*

LORIE.FINNIGHAN(3/17/2010 10:15:52 PM): *I saw that...you probably have not seen my email.*

LORIE.FINNIGHAN(3/17/2010 10:16:13 PM): *I wish I could help out here, but that is too much, Sweety, even for me*

CURTIS WELLS (3/17/2010 10:16:37 PM): *I have seen your email*

CURTIS WELLS (3/17/2010 10:17:40 PM): *well you know I am getting more profit from this so you bet I need to invest more*

LORIE.FINNIGHAN(3/17/2010 10:17:50 PM): *does that mean that you cannot come back until you have found that money*

LORIE.FINNIGHAN(3/17/2010 10:19:33 PM): *Curtis! talk to me*

CURTIS WELLS (3/17/2010 10:20:06 PM): *I need to pay that money before I leave here*

CURTIS WELLS (3/17/2010 10:20:15 PM): *I am here, sorry the connection is slow*

LORIE.FINNIGHAN(3/17/2010 10:20:35 PM): *okay, accepted*

LORIE.FINNIGHAN(3/17/2010 10:20:47 PM): *are you still missing the whole amount?*

CURTIS WELLS (3/17/2010 10:21:27 PM): *yes baby*

LORIE.FINNIGHAN(3/17/2010 10:21:42 PM): *don't you have partners in California or something*

CURTIS WELLS (3/17/2010 10:21:43 PM): *what I had, I will need to sort out Joshua's hospital bill*

LORIE.FINNIGHAN(3/17/2010 10:22:20 PM): *yep but surely you have insurance for the hospital bill*

CURTIS WELLS (3/17/2010 10:23:30 PM): *yes, I will get the money back from our international health insurance from California*

LORIE.FINNIGHAN(3/17/2010 10:24:00 PM): *How much is it?*

CURTIS WELLS (3/17/2010 10:24:05 PM): *you know that is what we are still using, and Obama is trying his best to help the US health care because it is really bad*

CURTIS WELLS (3/17/2010 10:24:41 PM): *you mean Joshua's hospital bill?*

LORIE.FINNIGHAN(3/17/2010 10:24:46 PM): *yes?*

CURTIS WELLS (3/17/2010 10:25:18 PM): *I will be given the bill by Friday*

LORIE.FINNIGHAN(3/17/2010 10:25:57 PM): *Webby, what am I going to do with you???? but I cannot be without you... so we are going to have to find a solution*

LORIE.FINNIGHAN(3/17/2010 10:26:17 PM): *so again, what about those partners of yours in California*

CURTIS WELLS (3/17/2010 10:26:31 PM): *well I cannot be without you too*

CURTIS WELLS (3/17/2010 10:26:49 PM): *they already invested their share in getting the pumps*

LORIE.FINNIGHAN(3/17/2010 10:27:25 PM): *aren't the pumps*

already committed to a contract?

CURTIS WELLS (3/17/2010 10:27:39 PM): *yes but they were bought*

LORIE.FINNIGHAN(3/17/2010 10:28:12 PM): *what I mean is that you said you already had a client for these pumps, right?*

CURTIS WELLS (3/17/2010 10:29:21 PM): *you know your role in the company right*

LORIE.FINNIGHAN(3/17/2010 10:29:28 PM): *no*

LORIE.FINNIGHAN(3/17/2010 10:29:33 PM): *I have a role in the company?*

CURTIS WELLS (3/17/2010 10:29:34 PM): *my better half*

LORIE.FINNIGHAN(3/17/2010 10:29:35 PM): *really?*

Curtis Wells (3/17/2010 10:29:50 PM): yes

LORIE.FINNIGHAN(3/17/2010 10:29:52 PM): *yep but Curtis, I don't print money in my basement*

LORIE.FINNIGHAN(3/17/2010 10:30:09 PM): *but hang on... I bought a lottery ticket for us today*

CURTIS WELLS (3/17/2010 10:30:25 PM): *really*

LORIE.FINNIGHAN(3/17/2010 10:31:02 PM): *weddings are expensive, Webby*

CURTIS WELLS (3/17/2010 10:31:36 PM): *it will be taken care of baby*

LORIE.FINNIGHAN(3/17/2010 10:32:55 PM): *look, what I can do is try to get a short-term loan for the 5K in your name but I will guarantee it, how do you feel about that?*

CURTIS WELLS (3/17/2010 10:33:30 PM): *well definitely I will pay it back when I leave here before leaving for California*

CURTIS WELLS (3/17/2010 10:33:40 PM): *how will you do that*

LORIE.FINNIGHAN(3/17/2010 10:33:43 PM): *WHAT!*

(3/17/2010 10:33:52 PM): *are you having me on*

LORIE.FINNIGHAN(3/17/2010 10:34:00 PM): *I saw that one coming*

LORIE.FINNIGHAN(3/17/2010 10:34:04 PM): *I am so mad at you*

CURTIS WELLS (3/17/2010 10:34:25 PM): *why baby I want to leave here and seriously I wish you where here*

LORIE.FINNIGHAN(3/17/2010 10:34:37 PM): *and go to*

California

CURTIS WELLS (3/17/2010 10:34:41 PM): *I will first come to Germany before going to California to clear the pumps*

CURTIS WELLS (3/17/2010 10:34:52 PM): *we can go together if you want*

CURTIS WELLS (3/17/2010 10:35:03 PM): *you think so Hollywood woman will steal your man*

LORIE.FINNIGHAN(3/17/2010 10:35:03 PM): *I have a full-time job Webby.*

LORIE.FINNIGHAN(3/17/2010 10:35:07 PM): *good job really*

LORIE.FINNIGHAN(3/17/2010 10:35:50 PM): *And YES... I know what those American chicks are like with all their silicon equipments*

CURTIS WELLS (3/17/2010 10:36:16 PM): *but you know I will have to go to California*

LORIE.FINNIGHAN(3/17/2010 10:36:26 PM): *well, thanks for sharing*

CURTIS WELLS (3/17/2010 10:36:34 PM): *I will really love you to come with me, it will be nice moving around together*

LORIE.FINNIGHAN(3/17/2010 10:36:37 PM): *I read that one between the lines in your email*

LORIE.FINNIGHAN(3/17/2010 10:37:09 PM): *sure but until that business of yours is putting food on the table, who is going to pay my mortgage, Webby?*

CURTIS WELLS (3/17/2010 10:37:50 PM): *ME*

LORIE.FINNIGHAN(3/17/2010 10:37:56 PM): *you are so cute*

LORIE.FINNIGHAN(3/17/2010 10:38:02 PM): *how...*

CURTIS WELLS (3/17/2010 10:38:03 PM): *I will get my cheque in the US*

LORIE.FINNIGHAN(3/17/2010 10:38:15 PM): *from whom/*

LORIE.FINNIGHANA(3/17/2010 10:38:23 PM): *you make me laugh*

LORIE.FINNIGHAN(3/17/2010 10:38:57 PM): *so when is it we are gong to California again? I need to buy a new bikini*

CURTIS WELLS (3/17/2010 10:39:24 PM): *really*

LORIE.FINNIGHAN(3/17/2010 10:39:43 PM): *yep! A really flashy, sexy one...*

CURTIS WELLS (3/17/2010 10:39:54 PM): *when I come to*

Germany I will be tracking the pumps to know when.

LORIE.FINNIGHAN (3/17/2010 10:40:55 PM): *oh and for Christmas, I want a new cleavage as well*

LORIE.FINNIGHAN(3/17/2010 10:41:21 PM): *they are very good in California apparently*

CURTIS WELLS (3/17/2010 10:43:00 PM): *you want to do breast augmentation?*

LORIE.FINNIGHAN(3/17/2010 10:43:52 PM): *slow down, here*

LORIE.FINNIGHAN(3/17/2010 10:43:58 PM): *I just want some restructuring*

LORIE.FINNIGHAN(3/17/2010 10:44:17 PM): *I am 45 Webby, not a young 20 something or did you miss that one*

LORIE.FINNIGHAN(3/17/2010 10:44:27 PM): *I call it asset management*

CURTIS WELLS (3/17/2010 10:46:15 PM): *you know I feel proud of you baby*

CURTIS WELLS (3/17/2010 10:46:31 PM): *baby can you still be online, I want to do some things*

LORIE.FINNIGHAN(3/17/2010 10:46:45 PM): *of course, Sweetheart*

CURTIS WELLS (3/17/2010 10:46:51 PM): *I will be back love*

CURTIS WELLS (3/17/2010 10:47:09 PM): *be right back*

As Curtis was showing no sign of coming back, Lorie decided to leave him a last message.

LORIE.FINNIGHAN(3/17/2010 11:30:58 PM): *Check your email... I need to go to bed now... you are driving me insane!!!!*

After they ended the conversation, Lorie sat back in her chair trying to process the wealth of information that had come through their exchanges. She was a little confused about why Curtis had not been upfront with her about having to go to California, although she had worked that one out well ahead of him telling her; she just was waiting to see how long it would take him to come clean with this plan.

9
April 3rd

For the following days, all Lorie did was to handle her professional dilemmas and to keep up with Curtis, because of Joshua. Eventually, the little man got released out of hospital, but, due to the fact that Curtis had to pay for the hospital bill, he was out of cash to meet up the last tax payment he needed to make so that he could leave. Lorie had asked him if his business associates could help him, but, again, she received a negative response.

At her wits end, and somewhat out of desperation, she agreed that she would advance him the five missing thousand euro so that Curtis and Joshua could leave Nigeria, but she ran into a hurdle at Western Union, which she discussed that evening with Curtis. She knew that she was taking a big risk by extending more cash to him but something was driving her and it was not all of his promises of a better life but something else. She could not quite figure it out.

CURTIS WELLS (3/27/2010 6:31:01 PM): *Hello baby*
CURTIS WELLS (3/27/2010 6:35:05 PM): *are you there honey*
CURTIS WELLS (3/27/2010 6:45:55 PM): *I miss you*
(3/27/2010 6:57:46 PM): *I am here Curtis*
CURTIS WELLS (3/27/2010 6:58:55 PM): *Hello Sweetheart*
LORIE.FINNIGHAN(3/27/2010 6:59:27 PM): *Curtis, we have a*

problem... I went to Western Union and they only let me transfer 2500 euro, which is 3000 USD

CURTIS WELLS (3/27/2010 7:00:09 PM): *you can do that twice*

CURTIS WELLS (3/27/2010 7:00:22 PM): *that is the best way to do that*

LORIE.FINNIGHAN(3/27/2010 7:01:29 PM): *no because my credit limit is as good as full now furthermore I have to send money to Jane so you will need to make do for now.*

CURTIS WELLS (3/27/2010 7:02:02 PM): *oh okay*

CURTIS WELLS (3/27/2010 7:02:10 PM): *can't you send more tomorrow?*

LORIE.FINNIGHAN(3/27/2010 7:02:11 PM): *but they asked me a lot of questions as this is the second time this months, I am sending you cash. I showed them the paper work but they would not accept that.*

CURTIS WELLS (3/27/2010 7:02:40 PM): *I understand, they have to 'cos they are looking out for you*

LORIE.FINNIGHAN(3/27/2010 7:02:50 PM): *My idea was to book the transfer on the visa which I will only have to pay after you are back.*

CURTIS WELLS (3/27/2010 7:03:18 PM): *oh okay, so what will you do then*

LORIE.FINNIGHAN(3/27/2010 7:03:26 PM): *I am so stressed out now as I got you to book your flight*

LORIE.FINNIGHAN(3/27/2010 7:03:48 PM): *is there any way those other guys of yours can pull the rest*

CURTIS WELLS (3/27/2010 7:04:35 PM): *I don't know baby, I can't promise and if I have to make any changes to the flight I will need to pay $100 fee or so*

LORIE.FINNIGHAN(3/27/2010 7:04:58 PM): *I feel awful did not see the issue with Western Union coming at all*

LORIE.FINNIGHAN(3/27/2010 7:05:22 PM): *okay, we need to get this solve 'cos you need to come back and I am not waiting another week*

CURTIS WELLS (3/27/2010 7:06:26 PM): *oh does that mean you can send one now and the other the next day or what*

LORIE.FINNIGHAN(3/27/2010 7:06:59 PM): *I have already sent 2500 today to you. You are not hearing me. I cannot do more transfers this month*

CURTIS WELLS (3/27/2010 7:09:00 PM): *I know you are stressed out already honey*

CURTIS WELLS (3/27/2010 7:09:06 PM): *I am sorry about that okay*

LORIE.FINNIGHAN (3/27/2010 7:09:50 PM): *this is for the tax payment right?*

CURTIS WELLS (3/27/2010 7:10:04 PM): *yes baby*

LORIE.FINNIGHAN(3/27/2010 7:10:28 PM): *well, they must have a bank account right?*

LORIE.FINNIGHAN(3/27/2010 7:12:43 PM): *Curtis we need to sort this out in the next couple of days. Is there anyone in California I could call on your behalf to get the rest? All they need is the other 50%*

CURTIS WELLS (3/27/2010 7:13:09 PM): *government thing, they do not do business like that here, are you thinking of sending them the rest*

CURTIS WELLS (3/27/2010 7:13:33 PM): *I know, I will see what I can do okay honey*

CURTIS WELLS (3/27/2010 7:13:46 PM): *but still do not understand why they will not allow you send the whole 5k*

LORIE.FINNIGHAN(3/27/2010 7:13:55 PM): *I feel very stressed and uncomfortable with all of this. Help me understand?*

CURTIS WELLS (3/27/2010 7:14:41 PM): *I was even going to tell you that you should send it twice 2500 each*

CURTIS WELLS (3/27/2010 7:14:55 PM): *but now I don't know what to say*

LORIE.FINNIGHAN(3/27/2010 7:15:08 PM): *I told you. There is a huge money laundry scams running currently in Nigeria so they have tightened up the regulations*

LORIE.FINNIGHAN3/27/2010 7:16:07 PM): *Curtis, why can't you send the tax payment later anyway?*

LORIE.FINNIGHAN(3/27/2010 7:17:53 PM): *Curtis... I am feeling frustrated and I have a tough time trying to understand. Help me out*

LORIE.FINNIGHAN(3/27/2010 7:29:34 PM): *Okay, so you are bailing out on me... That's pity... it is hardly my fault and I was looking forward to giving you the good news tonight*

LORIE.FINNIGHAN(3/27/2010 7:30:29 PM): *I cannot believe you just logged off*

She could not believe that Curtis logged out on her. It was in her eyes a very weak move on his part and decided to put his back against the wall by threatening him.

LORIE.FINNIGHAN (3/27/2010 7:34:41 PM): *if you want me to send you the Western Union ticket from today, .you better get back online*

LORIE.FINNIGHAN(3/27/2010 7:35:52 PM): *but it seems that football is more important than getting your son back into a decent place*

LORIE.FINNIGHAN(3/27/2010 7:46:38 PM): *Curtis. That's not fair you bailing out on me like this because we have an issue... The issue here is not the getting the money but getting it to you*

LORIE.FINNIGHAN(3/27/2010 7:47:11 PM): *Well, for someone who is so eager to have me in his arms, you have a funny way of showing it.*

She had suspected that although his status was showing him as being off line, he was watching her messages coming through one after the other.

CURTIS WELLS (3/27/2010 7:54:56 PM): *Hello baby*

CURTIS WELLS (3/27/2010 7:55:04 PM): *I didn't bail out on you baby, why will I do that*

LORIE.FINNIGHAN(3/27/2010 7:55:12 PM): *don't know*

CURTIS WELLS (3/27/2010 7:55:12 PM): *the computer froze and took me out*

LORIE.FINNIGHA(3/27/2010 7:55:27 PM): *God... I can not stand this anymore*

LORIE.FINNIGHAN(3/27/2010 7:55:43 PM): *You are coming back next week end and that's it*

CURTIS WELLS (3/27/2010 7:55:45 PM): *come on honey*

This was by far the most intense conversation they had ever had with each other. The frustration of getting Curtis to leave Nigeria so that they could finally meet up was getting to her really badly, but she was not prepared to back down and, through incredible manipulation, got the remaining cash to him in no time. Curtis had already made his plane reservation for the return, and the date had been set for April 3, finally.

For the next few days, all that they could discuss was what would happen next, and this was a very exciting and tense time for Lorie. She had not shared any of this with anyone except Sophie, but definitely had not said a word about Curtis' existence to her mother, as she did not need that pressure at that particular moment.

Lorie could not sleep on the night between the Saturday and Sunday, and woke up with a huge migraine as a result of it. The anticipation of going to the airport and meeting with Curtis face to face for the very first time was all too much for her, but, as she was walking the dogs that morning, she found ways to calm herself down somehow.

Curtis had given her a call the night before to let her know that they were on their way to the airport. She appreciated the gesture greatly, as she received it as a sign that the wheels were finally in motion.

As Lorie was standing at the airport holding her little dog, Lady, her heart was beating in anticipation of finally meeting, for the first time, the man she had shared so many evenings and nights chatting online to. The man she had found herself falling head over hills in love with without realising it. She stood away from the crowd, but still in a position where she could see the newly arrived passengers coming out of the luggage pick-up area, so that she could spot Curtis and Joshua coming out before he could see her, as she wanted to have a chance to compose herself before facing him for the very first time. Whilst screening the travellers coming out and observing them as they were being greeted, she was mentally reprocessing all that had gone on since she had first connected with Curtis. Within three months, she had connected with a total stranger online, developed a friendship that had grown into a business partnership, and now she was standing in an airport arrival lounge to pick up a man and a little boy who had become known to her as her family. Her life was seconds away from taking a brand-new turn, but she had no idea what it would look like.

She found herself brutally brought back out of her daze as she felt a tap on her shoulder, turned around and saw that one of the security staff was standing right behind her.

"Are you waiting for someone, Madam?" the lady asked.

"Well, have all the passengers from the Amsterdam flight debarked?" Lorie asked

"Yes, there is no one left," the lady said.

As those words were spoken, Lorie fell into a total state of shock, unable to move or breathe as her heart missed a beat or twenty in the process. After a few minutes just standing there like a discarded peace of luggage, she managed to control an incoming panic attack, recomposed herself, and ran out of the terminal building. She jumped in her car and drove back pedal to the metal, ignoring all road regulations to check if she had received a message of some sort.

There was no email or message on her answer phone. In total anger, as all she could think of was what the Western Union agent had told her about the Nigeria scams, she started to Google his name. Why didn't she think about that first?

Nothing came up from the initial Google search, so she

ran a trace on the US white pages website and came across a match. There was also a phone number, which she dialled without hesitation or even taking the time difference into consideration. A man answered. Not really knowing what to say, she put the phone down again. As she had just hung up, the device came to life again without warning, which made her jump out her chair. She grabbed the receiver as fast she could and pressed the 'answer' button.

"Hello, am I speaking to Lorie Wells?" a man's voice asked her

"Who are you?" she asked, her voice charged with anxiety.

"I am a doctor from Prestige Hospital in Lagos. Their taxi has had an accident and they are critical," the man answered.

"Who are you? Who are they? How did you get this number?" she shouted back to him.

"I am Dr. Devraw and your husband has had an accident," the man said calmly.

"You are lying…" she replied to him.

"I am not; your husband and your son are critical," the man insisted.

"What are their names?" Lorie asked in a defiant tone.

"Curtis and Joshua," the man answered immediately.

"I want to speak to Curtis," she demanded.

"He is not well right now; call back later," the man said.

Lorie felt as if the ground was cracking under her feet. How could this possibly happen? What was she to do now? As she was trying to put some order into her thoughts, she decided to let a couple of hours go by before picking up the phone to call the Los Angeles number again.

"Hello," said the man from earlier, in a grumpy voice.

"Hello, is Curtis Wells there? I need to speak to him," she asked hesitantly.

At this point, she had no idea with whom or what

exactly she was dealing with, and decided to assume that she had been well and truly scammed, but, before she went any further, she wanted to get confirmation of her suspicions.

"Sorry, who are you? And he is not here right now."

"Do you know when he will be back?" she asked.

"No, he is in Germany meeting up with some woman over there," the man said, somewhat irritated.

"Well, I am sorry to say that he is not."

"Who are you?" the man asked, getting more hostile as the conversation went on.

"Actually, I am Lorie, 'that woman', as you put it, and I have just received a phone call from Lagos informing me that they had a car crash last night."

"What are you telling me? How do you know this?"

"As I have just told you, some doctor from the hospital called me to inform me. Curtis had given him my number," she told the man, getting impatient.

"How can I reach him?" the man asked.

"If you give me your email address, I will send you the number. I have agreed with the hospital to call back this afternoon and I will let you know," Lorie said.

"Thank you. My email address is Chadlev@xxxxxx."

"Okay, thank you. I will send you an email if I get any news."

Having obtained the email address, she did not want to pressurise the stranger with too many questions at this stage. She would get back on to him eventually, as he was without doubt one of the partners Curtis had referred to, but would not use names. Later on in the afternoon, Lorie managed to speak to Curtis, who asked her to call someone by the name of Chad. She did not tell Curtis that she had already made contact with Chad, so as not to give him the sense that she has been researching him. For now, the only people on her mind were Curtis and Joshua, whom had been seriously injured. For them to get back to good enough health to be able to travel would, no doubt, take a couple of weeks, at least. Lorie exchanged regular emails with Chad, and she felt more comfortable about the fact that, on the surface, this was maybe not a scam, as communication between the three parties had become frequent and consistent.. All she could do, at this stage, was to wait again before she could finally meet up with the man who had apparently married her on the Internet without a judge, jury or priest even. The only question left to her was when? Or so she thought, as, now, she had no other option but to carry on in order to get to the bottom of it all. Completely frozen, she sat in her office staring blindly at the last email from Curtis.

To: loriefinnighan@xxxxxx
From:curtiswells62@xxxxxx
Subject: My Heart is yours
Date: Saturday , April 2.2010 11.15pm

Hello, Sweetheart,

I have already done everything and now we are set; I have gone to the officials and made the payment; also had to complete it... I will call you when we are about to leave for the airport, okay. Joshua is excited and asking me if he can take something from Nigeria, so we will go and check out some local sculpture, or maybe a painting, I am sure you will like it, 'cos I found some that were really nice and I think I will like it.

I can't wait for tomorrow, baby; I can't wait to have my woman for the rest of my life; tomorrow will be the start of a new day for me and I will be like a newborn baby when planting that kiss on you, and I am so excited, honey, and I cant contain myself.
1-4-3 Forever and always. Remember that.
Your hubby.

143 – More Than LIFE
Prologue

Hi, Lorie,

How are you doing? I have just been able to read all the emails you sent to me... Since last Wednesday, I have been in the hospital, because I have not been feeling too well. I am having problems with my credit union, because of the loans I owe. I have not heard from Curtis; I do not know what is wrong, because he was supposed to contact me so that I can go and get the money from the bank.

He had already told them that the tax company will release the funds once they get their money and signed that I can go and get it, but when I got to the bank today I was told that the tax people in UK have not contacted them; that means Curtis is nowhere to be found if you say you have sent him the money, and he was supposed to be in Germany.

I am really worried and scared right now; I have a lot of things going on and, in fact, this could really ruin my life, and I am also taking care of Joshua.

Please, Lorie, let me know what is going on, because I am confused.

Stay blessed,
Chad.

Breinigsville, PA USA
21 March 2011
258106BV00003B/18/P